THE
Winner
IS...

NEXT BEST JUNIOR CHEF

EPISODE 3

THE Winner IS...

by **Charise Mericle Harper**

with illustrations by **Aurélie Blard-Quintard**

HOUGHTON MIFFLIN HARCOURT
Boston   New York

hmhbooks.com

The text was set in Garamond Premier Pro.
Illustrations by Aurélie Blard-Quintard

The Library of Congress has cataloged the hardcover edition as follows:
Names: Harper, Charise Mericle, author. | Blard-Quintard, Aurelie,
illustrator.
Title: The winner is... / by Charise Mericle Harper ; with illustrations by
Aurâelie Blard-Quintard .
Description: Boston ; New York : Houghton Mifflin Harcourt, [2018] | Series:
Next Best Junior Chef ; 3 | Summary: The finalists face surprises as they
find their culinary knowledge, ingenuity, and friendship tested in the
final week of competition that will determine who earns the title of Next
Best Junior Chef.
Identifiers: LCCN 2018019094
Subjects: | CYAC: Cooking—Fiction. | Contests—Fiction. |
Television—Production and direction—Fiction. | Friendship—Fiction. |
BISAC: JUVENILE FICTION / Cooking & Food. | JUVENILE FICTION / Action &
Adventure / General. | JUVENILE FICTION / Humorous Stories. | JUVENILE
FICTION / Performing Arts / Television & Radio. | JUVENILE FICTION / Media
Tie-In. | JUVENILE FICTION / Business, Careers, Occupations.
Classification: LCC PZ7.H231323 Win 2018 | DDC [Fic]—dc23
LC record available at https://lccn.loc.gov/2018019094

ISBN: 978-0-544-99144-6 paper over board
ISBN: 978-1-328-55902-9 paperback

Printed in the United States of America
DOC 10 9 8 7 6 5 4 3 2 1
4500748434

This book is dedicated to adventurous eaters.
I don't know who the first person was to
think of eating an artichoke, but thank you.
They are delicious!

CHAPTER 1

Caroline turned away from the studio door and studied Rae's face. "Friends . . ."

". . . to the end!" They finished the sentence together. After two tough weeks of slicing and dicing, they were the only ones left. This was it! Now it was the battle to see who would be the winner.

"Shhhhh." Chef Nancy put a finger to her lips.

Rae rubbed her palms against her shirt. In just a few seconds the door would open and it would begin all over again.

Rae counted the days on her fingers and then wiped her hands on her skirt. In seven days one of them would be the winner—the Next Best Junior Chef! And the other . . . She didn't want to think about that. She studied the back of Caroline's head. Was she nervous about winning or—worse— losing? The producer's voice interrupted her thoughts.

"BOOMS!"

"LIGHTS!"

"CAMERAS!"

"ROLLING!"

And then the announcer began. "Welcome to *Next Best Junior Chef*! This is week three, our FINAL week of competition. After Thursday's elimination round, we'll have a winner for the Next Best Junior Chef! We have two remaining talented junior chefs, who have certainly earned the right to be here, but are they ready for what lies ahead? This week's challenges will test their culinary knowledge, ingenuity, and maybe even the bonds of their friendship. It's time to jump from the frying pan into the fire. Will they sizzle or fizzle? We can't wait to find out—so without further delay, let's bring out our final contestants."

Chef Nancy tapped Caroline's shoulder. Caroline walked confidently to the front of the studio, pacing herself to match the announcer's tempo.

"Congratulations, Caroline, and welcome to this exciting final week of competition. Caroline is eleven years old and from Chicago, Illinois. She worked some fast-food magic last week, elevating a hot dog to an *haute* dog. She has continually impressed the judges with her creativity and culinary talent."

Chef Nancy held the door for Rae.

"Congratulations, Rae, and welcome to the final week of competition."

Rae blinked twice, focused on the front, and started down the ramp. The energy of the room quickly changed her nervousness into excitement.

"Rae is eleven years old and from Port Chester, New York. Last week, she won unanimous praise for perfecting a cookie classic and served up a winning dish in the elimination round. This young chef is a master of both pleasing the palate and presentation."

Rae stood next to Caroline in front of the three judges.

"Our esteemed judges include Chef Vera Porter of the famous Porter Farm Restaurant, the renowned pastry chef Aimee Copley, and Chef Gary Lee, restaurant proprietor and host of the award-winning show *Adventures in Cooking*. The judges will be watching our competitors throughout the week, and everything that happens along the way will be taken into consideration when we get to the final elimination round. In addition to choosing a winner, the judges will have to dismiss one of our junior chefs and ask them to hang up their apron. This decision will be based on performance, the taste and presentation of their dishes, and their overall creative vision."

Caroline reached for Rae's hand, then gave it a squeeze and held on. Rae squeezed back.

"Our junior chefs are mentored by Chef Nancy Patel, the 2013 recipient of the Golden Spoon Award. The winner of *Next Best Junior Chef* will receive two life-changing prizes: a custom food truck *and* a guest spot on *Adventures in Cooking*  when it begins filming this summer in Italy!"

Chef Gary stepped to the center of the room. "WOW! This is it!" He nodded to each of the junior chefs. "Congratulations. You've made it!"

They smiled back.

He shook his head. "I have to be honest, this is not going to be an easy week, but"—he raised a finger—"it will be exciting. We have twists, turns, and *lots* of surprises. You will not be disappointed. As in previous weeks, there is a theme, and we're especially excited about this one. Our theme for the week is innovation. So we'll want to see some fresh new ideas. Are you ready to battle it out and flex your creative muscles?"

"YES, CHEF!"

"And you're still friends?" He pointed to their joined hands. "Remarkable! Well, that calls for a celebration. Let's have a toast!" He motioned to an assistant standing at the side of the studio. "Bring out the champagne!"

CHAPTER 2

Champagne? Rae looked worried, Caroline confused. They weren't old enough to drink champagne!

Chef Aimee laughed. "Don't worry, it's not champagne. We have something even more special. Any guesses?"

"Sparkling apple juice."

"Ginger ale?"

A stagehand pushed a rolling cart with six fancy glasses to the front of the room. Caroline frowned. It definitely wasn't ginger ale.

Chef Aimee handed out the glasses. "Chef Porter has prepared one of her favorite chilled soups for this occasion, and she'll lead us in the toast."

Rae studied the glass. The soup was light green with one perfectly cut square crouton floating on top.

Chef Porter raised her glass. "Congratulations to you both, and may our final week be one of discoveries."

Chef Gary emptied his glass in one gulp, chewed up the

crouton, then nodded to Chef Porter. "Thank you, Chef, for that refreshing start to the week." He turned back to the junior chefs, a smile on his face. "Are you ready for fun?"

They nodded. Caroline winced and forced herself to swallow. The soup tasted like soap. That meant only one thing—cilantro! Two weeks ago, Chef Nancy had told the junior chefs about the gene that makes cilantro taste like soap. People are just born with it; they can't help it. Caroline was one of those people.

Chef Gary clapped his hands. "Great! Glad to hear it . . . because the fun starts now! RIGHT NOW!"

"WHAT?" Rae covered her mouth, but it was too late. Everyone had heard.

Chef Gary wagged his finger. "See, I told you there'd be surprises. Your first challenge is to create a fun, easy dish composed of the flavors you just tasted in this soup. Don't worry, there'll be more samples at your workstations, so you can try it again."

Caroline suppressed a groan. More soup equaled *more* soap!

"And . . ." Chef Gary pointed a finger. "Please keep a list of every ingredient you use. We'll need that list when you come to the table at the end of the challenge. You'll have a total of thirty minutes for this challenge. Five minutes at your workstations for a pantry list, five minutes in the pantry, and then twenty minutes to prepare your final creation." He raised his hand. "Your time starts now—GO!"

Caroline and Rae raced off to their workstations. One was smiling; the other was not.

CAROLINE

This challenge is not going to be easy. I have this gene thing that makes cilantro taste like soap. I can't help it—I was just born that way. I'm going to have to force myself to drink it and see if I can figure out any of the other flavors. Just by the color and the texture, I'm guessing the main ingredient is avocado. I can't believe we are starting the competition so soon and I'm already at a disadvantage.

RAE

The fast start was a real surprise, but I'm ready for it. I actually really liked the soup. Cilantro is one of my favorite flavors, so that was easy to pick out. Plus the flavor profile was a little spicy, so I'm guessing there is some kind of pepper in there too. It's tricky with a blended soup—you can't see the ingredients. But we get to taste it again, so that's going to be helpful. Poor Caroline! She is not going to like this challenge, and I don't blame her. Who wants to drink a mouthful of soup!

CHAPTER 3

Rae took a sip of soup, and then quickly added corn and lime juice to her list. Figuring out the ingredients was easier than she thought it would be. She wiggled her tongue. *Thank you, tongue!* She was lucky—she had a sophisticated palate. The roasted corn was a good catch—there was only a hint of the charred smoky flavor, but she'd caught it. She looked over the ingredients on her list. Now came the fun part: deciding what to make.

Caroline wasn't so lucky—spicy soap was the best she could do. The soaplike cilantro taste overpowered everything. She'd tried, but after three mouthfuls, she was done. She sighed and looked for visual clues instead. The pale green color meant the avocado was mixed with other ingredients—probably vegetable broth and something white. She scribbled down a guess: sour cream.

"TIME!" Chef Gary stood at the front of the room; a second later he shouted again. "PANTRY RUN!"

Janet and Mike followed Caroline and Rae to the pantry with their cameras. They filmed Rae grabbing two ears of corn, limes, serrano chiles, and garlic, and then closed in for a close-up of Caroline at the spice wall. She frowned, hesitated, and then added smoked paprika, pepper, celery salt, cumin, salt, and ancho chili pepper to her basket. She was shopping blind—no recipe, no idea what to make. Her only plan was to grab everything she might need and decide later.

"WORKSTATIONS!"

"CUT!" The cameras turned off.

Caroline was grateful for the extra time. Since she couldn't figure out all the ingredients, she'd have to wow the judges in a different way. Her presentation on the plate would have to be amazing.

Chef Nancy came by to visit as the junior chefs unpacked their groceries. Sometimes she offered suggestions, but mostly she provided reassurance. She tried not to look worried, but she knew about Caroline's trouble with cilantro. "How is it going?"

Caroline held up a perfectly ripe avocado. "I have a plan—baked avocados in the half shell."

"Oooh! Intriguing."

"And delicious!"

Rae saw Chef Nancy approaching and waved her over. "I was inspired by the crouton, so I'm going to make avocado toast and incorporate all the flavors of the soup."

Chef Nancy raised her arms. "I give up. You two don't need me." She wiped away a pretend tear, and then touched her heart. "I'm so proud . . . of both of you!"

The junior chefs grinned, first at Chef Nancy, then each other. It was a perfect start to the competition.

"ROLLING!"

Chef Aimee stood in the center of the room with her arm in the air. "LET'S GET COOKING!"

"Do the corn first!" Rae talked to herself as she worked. She shucked the corn and then rubbed it with olive oil. Grilling on the stove was harder than grilling on a barbecue—the flame was closer. "Ouch!" She pulled the corn off the gas burner, grabbed some tongs, and slowly rotated the ear above the flame. This wasn't the best use of her time, but she had no choice. Charred and burned are very different flavors.

Caroline did the math in her head. Twenty minutes minus twelve minutes in the oven meant there were only eight minutes left, and that needed to be split up between prepping and plating. She had to rush! She halved an avocado, removed the pit, and scooped out the flesh, careful not to damage the skin.

Chef Gary approached just as she was mixing up the filling. "Everything okay?"

She nodded but didn't look up. She was too busy to chat.

"What are you mixing up?"

Caroline sighed and put down her spoon. "Avocado, feta cheese, onions, and pepper, and if I don't get this into those"—she pointed to two empty avocado shells—"I'm going to be in trouble."

Chef Gary nodded. "Don't worry about me, I'm just observing."

Caroline filled the first shell, piling it high, then set it on a baking tray. It tipped and fell to the side, spilling the filling onto the tray. "Nooo!" She replaced the filling and set it upright. It tipped again.

Chef Gary shook his head. "Some things can't stand alone." He turned to leave, then added, "I'd think about that."

Caroline repeated his words and then looked back at the tray. *Together! That was the opposite of alone!* She almost shouted a thank-you, but Chef Gary was already gone. She quickly added filling to another shell and then balanced the two shells together. Seconds later the tray was in the oven.

The judges want us to succeed. I don't think getting help is cheating. They help everyone. It's not like Chef Gary told me exactly what to do. He just nudged me to think of my problem in a different way. I came up with the answer.

CAROLINE

CHAPTER 4

Caroline and Rae started the last fifteen minutes with the same worry: time!

Caroline set the temperature to 375 degrees, hoping a hotter oven would compensate for less time.

Rae set the ears on a plate. The grilling had taken a lot longer than she'd planned. She was way behind schedule.

Chef Gary studied her bare countertop. "What's going on here?"

"Buttered corn. First, I'm slicing the kernels off the cob. The butter is mixed with smoked paprika, salt, and pepper, so the flavors meld. Then, I'll toss the kernels in the butter mixture. I know, there's a lot to do, but I do have a plan." Rae counted off on her fingers: "Toast, avocados, and plating." She grabbed a loaf of seeded bread and cut off two fat slices. "See?"

"Absolutely," agreed Chef Gary. "Go to it."

"FIVE MINUTES!"

Rae opened her oven door and flipped the bread. Two minutes under the broiler and it'd be done.

Caroline opened her oven door and then closed it again. Two minutes of cooking and then time to plate.

Rae spread the avocado mash onto the freshly toasted bread, added two spoonfuls of the buttered corn, then sprinkled on queso fresco and chopped cilantro. A pinch of smoked paprika added a final dash of color. At the last minute she added a wedge of lime.

Caroline placed her half avocado in the center of a plate, held her breath, and then slowly let go. It was balancing, but only barely. She drizzled a zigzag pattern of sriracha mayonnaise on top, and added a sprinkling of breadcrumbs. The final decoration was a sprig of cilantro.

"TIME!"

Caroline and Rae stepped back from their workstations, hands in the air.

"CUT."

The cameras were off.

Caroline studied her plate. Was the avocado starting to tip to the side, or was that just her imagination?

Caroline and Rae stood next to each other, off to the side, while the cameras moved in to film their plates.

"Nice presentation!" whispered Rae, and then suddenly her smile faded.

Caroline spun around. What? What had she seen? "Noooooo." A slow moan escaped her lips. Caroline's avocado was lying on its side, and the filling had spilled everywhere— the plate, the table, and even the floor. It was a disaster!

Chef Nancy rushed over to the plate, motioned for Steve, and called to the judges. Rae watched the group talking and gesturing. She leaned toward Caroline. "I'm so sorry!"

Caroline stared at the ground, rhythmically repeating the same three words, over and over. *Do not cry. Do not cry. Do not cry.* Suddenly she was looking at a pair of feet. Chef Nancy touched her shoulder.

"Don't worry. We're going to work this out, It was Mark, the cameraman. He accidentally nudged your plate."

Caroline looked up. "He did?"

"Yes! So, we're going to give you time to fix it. To restore it to how it was before. I noticed you baked another avocado. You may use that one instead. The judges have agreed that it would be fair." She gently nudged Caroline forward. "Come on, you can work on it now."

Five minutes later a new avocado was on a new plate, looking exactly like the original.

Mark the cameraperson rushed over to take some close-ups. He stopped two feet before the table, then stepped forward cautiously. "Caroline, I'm very sorry about what happened. I'll be careful, I promise."

Caroline nodded but stayed silent. She definitely didn't say what she was thinking. *Thank you, Mark—I'm glad you bumped it. This second avocado is a lot more stable. That first avocado was probably going to fall anyway.*

When Mark was done, Caroline and Rae moved back to their workstations and the judges returned to the front of the room.

Chef Gary stepped forward. "Before we continue I want to make sure that you're both okay with what just happened.

I know the extra wait means that we will not be trying your dishes in the best of circumstances. Things might have gotten soggy and cold when you intended them to be crispy and hot. This will all be taken into account. You will not lose points for anything related to the delay. Are you okay with that?"

Caroline looked at Rae. Rae nodded. "Yes, Chef."

RAE

What was I supposed to say? Is it unfair? Maybe. Caroline's avocado was going to fall over. I could tell— it was leaning. All the cameraman did was make it happen sooner than later. So, she got a lucky break. Good for her, but I don't have to be happy about it.

CHAPTER 5

Rae tried to shrug off the disappointment, but it wasn't easy. Caroline's plating was better than hers. What was going to happen now? Did she even have a chance?

Steve waved his arm. "ROLLING."

Chef Gary looked into the camera. "We gave our two young chefs a surprise start. This was not an easy challenge, but they stepped up and delivered. Well done."

Chef Porter's gaze settled on Caroline. "Caroline, will you please bring your plate to the table?"

Caroline slowly walked forward. One avocado disaster was enough, and if it happened again, she wouldn't get another redo. She carefully set the plate down, relieved.

Chef Porter was instantly impressed. "Lovely! What a creative presentation. Caroline, what have you made us?"

"I made a stuffed avocado with a spicy sriracha mayonnaise."

"Should we try it?" Chef Aimee held up three forks.

NEXT BEST JUNIOR CHEF

"Nice crunch with the breadcrumbs."

"Not too spicy on the sauce—just the right amount of bite."

"The avocado pairs nicely with the feta, and you managed the salt perfectly. Not everyone remembers that feta is a salty cheese."

Suddenly, Chef Porter was wearing her pickle face—the expression that looked like she'd just bitten into a very sour pickle.

Caroline shuddered—this was bad.

The frown deepened. "Something's missing . . . something important." Chef Porter paused. "Cilantro! Where's the cilantro?"

Chef Aimee pointed to the decorative sprig that had been pushed to the side of the plate.

Chef Gary shook his head. "I see it, but I'm not tasting it."

Chef Porter poked at the sprig. "Well, we might as well move on."

Chef Aimee called Rae to the table.

Caroline turned to leave, but Chef Porter stopped her. "Caroline, you may stay at the front, but please move over to the side."

Rae set her dish down. The mood around the table had changed. Five minutes ago she'd been excited, but now she was nervous.

Chef Porter smiled. "Rae, what have you made us?"

"I made *elote* avocado toast with a spicy relish."

"Dig in." Chef Gary scooped up a bite. "Ah, cilantro! There it is."

Chef Porter agreed. "Yes, and I'm especially happy to see the grilled corn. I wasn't sure if anyone was going to pick that out. Very clever."

Rae relaxed and the judges continued.

"The crunch of the toast and the smoothness of the avocado is a nice contrast."

"It's nicely spicy. It could be too much, but the queso fresco mellows it out."

Chef Gary squeezed some lime on his second bite. "That's the tang I was looking for. Well done, Rae." He turned to the other judges. "Shall we confer to—"

"The ingredient lists," interrupted Chef Porter. "Please hand them in."

Chef Gary read off the list of ingredients in the soup. "Avocados, corn, garlic, onion, serrano chile, lime juice, créma, cilantro, olive oil, water, crouton, and salt." He waved the ingredient lists from the junior chefs. "We'll see how many of these you covered."

Rae waited until Chef Gary was at the back of the room with the other chefs; she leaned closer to Caroline and nudged her arm. Caroline didn't respond. Rae couldn't blame her—disappointing Chef Porter never felt good.

Minutes later the judges were back and Chef Gary was talking.

"This was not an easy challenge. We surprised you, and tested you in a new and unfamiliar way. Caroline, your dish was original and exceptionally creative, but you were missing one of the main ingredients of the soup. Quite frankly, that was a surprise and a disappointment. A garnish is not a valid representation of an essential flavor."

Caroline lowered her head, wishing the floor would swallow her up, but this was a cooking show: the only magic that happened here was with food.

Chef Porter waved a piece of paper. "I have the tally. One

young chef incorporated eight of my ingredients; the other had five."

Chef Gary continued. "Plus the texture and combination of flavors in the winning dish was spot on. Congratulations, Rae, you are the winner of this challenge! Please come to the front. We all enjoyed your avocado toast. I could see serving something like this with an egg on it for breakfast. In fact, I might even try it this weekend."

Rae walked forward to stand with the judges. At first it was exciting, the clapping and the accolades, but then something happened. Seeing Caroline across the table, alone with her head down, took all the fun away. And there was a new realization—this wasn't just going to be hard on the loser. It was going to be hard on their friendship, too.

This is not the way I wanted to start the week, but I'm not discouraged. I had a huge disadvantage in this challenge, but I did okay. I may have missed the cilantro, but the judges loved my presentation and that's a win, because Rae is a tough competitor when it comes to plating. If not for the cilantro—and that's not my fault—I would have won!

CAROLINE

CHAPTER 6

Caroline and Rae were back at Porter Lodge on Chef Porter's farm, surrounded by acres of forest. They sprawled out on the big soft armchairs in the main room.

Rae leaned back against the pillows. "I don't know why I'm so tired. We've been doing this for two weeks, and now after only one challenge . . . I'm exhausted."

Caroline stretched her arms. "Me too. Do you think it was the surprise of it? You know, because we weren't expecting a challenge?"

"Maybe." Rae closed her eyes. "I bet that's how the whole week will be—surprise after surprise. We'll have to expect the unexpected."

Caroline threw a pillow to the floor. "Ugh. I don't even want to think about it. Let's talk about something else."

They were silent for a moment, and then Caroline sat up. "Hey, you didn't get to go to the Gadget Wall." Nearly every day for the past two weeks of competition, the junior chefs had been adding fun cooking gadgets to their personal toolboxes every time they won a challenge—spinners, slicers, strainers, mezzalunas, spiralizers, citrus presses. Anything a junior chef could want in her dream kitchen. But today there'd been no Gadget Wall.

Now Rae sat up too. "You're right. I wonder why. Is it still there? Did you see it?"

Caroline chewed on her finger. "I don't know. I didn't notice."

Chef Nancy stood in the doorway of the main room. "How is everyone doing? I know that was a big surprise today, but you both handled it well."

Rae eyed the papers in Chef Nancy's hand. Was that the schedule for the week?

Chef Nancy sat down across from Rae and Caroline and glanced at the papers. "The only thing left for today is an interview with Steve the producer, and then tomorrow we have a morning field trip. We'll leave right at eight."

Caroline put her hand out for a schedule, but Chef Nancy pulled them close. "I'll hang on to these until after the field trip. We'll go over everything tomorrow."

"Where are we going?" Rae offered a half smile, but she already knew the answer.

Chef Nancy looked apologetic. "I'm sorry, I can't tell you."

"More surprises!" Caroline swung her hand into the air. "Every day will be an adventure."

Chef Nancy stood up. "That's the spirit. If you're open to anything, you'll be ready for everything."

Caroline nodded. Words of wisdom from Chef Nancy felt good—even if you didn't really believe them.

Rae waited until Chef Nancy was out of the room. "What was that? Now I'm even more confused. Surprise start, no schedule, and no Gadget Wall! That's all different. What's going on?"

Caroline shrugged. Could a shrug be a lie? No, not if it was only a feeling. Something about tomorrow's field trip was going to be a BIG surprise.

RAE

I'm excited about this week, because both Caroline and I are serious competitors. We don't play games. This will be about cooking only, and when we're not in the kitchen, we're friends. I trust her and she trusts me. It's not easy to battle against a friend, but we can do it and still have fun.

I'm excited about this week, because Rae and I understand each other. We know the other's strengths and weaknesses. That makes this an even match. We'll each do our best, and the best chef will win.

CAROLINE

CHAPTER 7

C hef Nancy rushed through the room, but stopped when she saw Caroline and Rae at the breakfast table. "Good morning, junior chefs! Big day today." She pointed to the door. "Ten minutes and we'll be leaving in the van."

Rae grabbed a muffin off the table and watched Caroline. Would she choose sugared cereal, again, like every day for the past two weeks? Or was that being *too* superstitious?

Caroline paused at the cereal, then moved on. "Sorry, cereal, I can't do it!" She picked up a muffin.

Rae laughed. "It can't hear you. It doesn't have feelings."

"I know, but we had a thing going. What if cereal in the morning was my *lucky charm* for the competition?"

"HA! Nice pun, but I don't believe in luck, at least not that kind."

Caroline took a bite of muffin and closed her eyes. "Mmm—me neither, and this tastes soooo much better."

Chef Nancy was a stickler about time. Ten minutes later, they were in the van and heading off on the mystery field trip.

"How long until we get there?" asked Caroline.

Chef Nancy looked at her phone. "About ninety minutes."

"Good to know." Rae leaned back and closed her eyes. "I'll start worrying in eighty minutes."

....

Rae slept on and off for the first thirty minutes, and then she was fast asleep. She awoke with a start as soon as the van stopped.

"We're here!" Caroline opened her door and jumped out.

Rae blinked and tried to focus. "WHAT? Why did you let me sleep so long?" But no one was left to answer. She stumbled out the door. Where were they? It took a few moments for her eyes to adjust to the bright morning light. Who was that in the distance? Chef Gary and Chef Aimee?

Caroline moved next to her. "Cranberries."

"Is that some kind of code?" Rae's brain felt foggy.

"NO, silly! It's a fruit. This is a cranberry farm."

Rae shot Caroline a nasty glare. Why hadn't she woken her up? But Caroline was too excited to notice. "I think it's kind of cool. I don't know anything about cranberries—do you? Cranberry challenge . . . that's not so hard, right?" She playfully pushed Rae's arm. "I was worried for nothing."

"Junior chefs, stand here!" Steve pointed to a spot on the grass.

Chef Gary and Chef Aimee moved over to face them.

Rae looked around. What was she missing? Cranberries couldn't be the big surprise. There had to be something else. But what?

RAE

I can't believe Caroline didn't wake me up. She's not like me—she doesn't think about the big picture. There might have been clues on the drive in, and now we missed them. Chef Nancy didn't mention that the judges would be here—that's huge. Something *big* is going on.

CHAPTER 8

Chef Gary got started as soon as the cameras were rolling. "Welcome, junior chefs. As you can see, we're here at a cranberry farm. I'm excited for you to learn about one of America's most interesting fruits, but . . ." He held up a finger. "Before we begin, we have a little surprise that—"

"Big surprise," interrupted Chef Aimee. She was smiling at something in the distance.

Rae shuddered. What was it? A something, or a someone? She couldn't see.

"Eyes on me," instructed Chef Gary. "We'll show you in a moment, but first I want you to know that we have given this a lot of thought, and were this you, in a different pair of shoes, you'd be happy for the opportunity. Remember, the best chef is going to win this competition, no matter what. Can you win this?"

"YES, CHEF!"

Rae froze. She and Caroline weren't the only ones shouting. Tate and Oliver raced forward and stepped up next to Chef Gary.

TATE

How did I feel when they told me I had another chance to get back on the show? I did jumping jacks! I can't wait for this next challenge so I can show the judges all I've got! Being the first contestant to go home in week one was tough—but I am tougher!

OLIVER

> Sure, I lost the elimination challenge in week two, but I don't want to talk about that. As soon as Steve the producer called, I was ready. I'm back and I'm here to stay! I'm going to win this challenge. The world's going to see that I deserve to be the Next Best Junior Chef.

Caroline gasped. "What? They get to come back?"

"*Only* if one of them wins this challenge," cautioned Chef Aimee.

Caroline looked like she was about to burst into tears.

Rae's hands tightened into fists. This wasn't fair. They'd already beaten them!

Steve stood off to the side, smiling. This was his kind of moment: tension, surprise, and anger. This was good television.

Chef Gary furrowed his brow and nodded sympathetically. "Here's how it's going to work. Later today, there'll be a challenge, and the winner of that challenge will win a prize. However, if the winner of the challenge is either Tate or Oliver, they will forgo the prize and instead win the right to compete again as a contestant in the competition, right through to the end of this week to the final winner-take-all challenge."

The cameraperson moved in for some close-ups. Two faces were smiling and two were scowling.

Rae's hand shot up. "So if they lose today, they are out—FOREVER?"

"Yes, forever." Chef Gary motioned for Tate and Oliver to join Caroline and Rae in the lineup. "Junior chefs, I'm happy to offer you this new opportunity, and to sweeten the pot, Chef Aimee will tell you about the prize."

Chef Aimee held up a card. "The winner of this challenge will win a dinner for four at Le Soupir."

Caroline tugged on Rae's arm. "That's in Paris! France!"

Chef Aimee continued. "Le Soupir is of course the most celebrated five-star restaurant in Paris, France. So in addition to the dinner, you will also win transportation and a three-night hotel stay in one of the foodie-est cities in the world!"

The corners of Rae's lips slowly curled up—she couldn't help it. She'd love to take her grandma to Paris. This was a great prize, and beating Oliver again would be the bonus.

Caroline grinned. "Le Soupir!" If she won, her mom would have a heart attack. Well, not *really*. But she dreamed about that restaurant.

Chef Gary looked over the group. "Four smiling faces. I knew we'd get there. Well, enjoy your morning, and we'll see you back in the studio for your challenge. Are you ready for a big day?"

"YES, CHEF!" The response was unanimous.

"CUT!"

RAE

I can't believe what just happened. Is it fair? I guess it doesn't matter what I think, but I'm not worried. I beat them before, so I can beat them again. Really, this is more like Caroline and me against Oliver and Tate. We have to win, so it can go back to being just the two of us!

Wow! I don't know what to talk about first. Oliver and Tate being back is big, but Le Soupir! That's huge! My mom has been talking about that restaurant forever! Of course, we would never get to go there—it's super expensive and it takes more than a year to secure a reservation, *and* it's in another country. I can't believe it. I really want to get this for my mom. I will win this!

CAROLINE

OLIVER

I don't care about the fancy restaurant. I just need to get back in this game. I messed up once, but I won't mess up again. Second chances are for setting the record straight, and that's what I'm going to do. I'm going all the way to the end, and I'm going to win!

TATE

Of course, I feel lucky to be back. I thought Caroline and Rae would be more happy to see us, but I guess it makes sense that they aren't. They don't want us to win. I get it, but I'm grateful to have another chance. I'm ready to prove that I deserve to be here.

CHAPTER 9

hef Nancy let everyone have fifteen minutes to chat and get reacquainted. There were a few seconds of awkwardness, and then there were hugs—almost all around. It was okay. Oliver wasn't a huggy person.

"This way!" Chef Nancy led the group toward a large metal building. As they got closer, two men came out to meet them.

Tate poked Oliver in the arm. "They're wearing fishing pants! Maybe we'll go fishing?"

Chef Nancy stopped the group. "Junior chefs, this is Mr. Rumez and Mr. Dumkirk. They are the owners and partners of this farm, and today they're going to teach us about one of America's original fruits: the cranberry."

Mr. Rumez stepped forward. "Please, call me David, and this is Ben. We're a little new to cranberry farming. We've only been here for ten years, but we love it."

Tate leaned in to Rae. "That's older than me."

She smiled. Not liking Tate was impossible!

Ben studied the group. "We're also kind of new to giving tours. So we've come up with two choices. Number one: We can go inside and watch an exciting video about cranberries and then answer your questions. Or number two: You can all put on a pair of these and have some fun!" He pointed to his fishing pants.

"TWO! TWO!" Tate bounced up and down, and then turned to plead with the others. "Can we? Please! Don't choose the video!"

"Pants!" agreed Oliver.

Caroline and Rae nodded.

"PANTS FOR THE WIN!" Tate high-fived the air.

RAE

This was one of the best tours we've ever been on. A bog is like a shallow swimming pool, only it's as big as a field. The cranberries grow on vines at the bottom, and when it's picking season, they flood the bog with water. A special machine drives through the bog and shakes the vines, and all the cranberries float to the top. Red berries floating on water look amazing.

The special pants are not easy to walk in, and they aren't just pants. They're rubber boots attached to rubber overalls. It's like wearing half a space suit. But once you get in the water with them, it's worth it. It's easier to move around. It's a good thing I've been doing squats—that helped a lot.

TATE

Ben led the group behind the building and down a small path. He pointed to the sunken fields on either side of them. "As you can see, these bogs aren't flooded with water. It's too soon in the season—the plants haven't yet produced their fruit. We'll flood these in the fall, when the fruit is mature, and then again in December to protect the plants from the cold over winter. But don't worry—you haven't missed all the fun. We have something special coming right up."

"WOW!" Caroline stopped and stared. "It's beautiful."

A bog the size of a large swimming pool was filled with water and brightly colored cranberries. David held up a cranberry. "Anyone know why these float?"

Oliver's hand shot up. "They're lighter than water!"

"Right!" David broke open the berry and passed it around. "They have small air chambers inside, and because of this, we can harvest the fruit without damaging the plant."

Ben held up a net. "Now let's catch some cranberries."

When it's harvest time, they use big machines to scoop up the cranberries, but since this was just for fun, we used nets and buckets. David said it wasn't a race, but Oliver was pretty competitive. He filled up seven buckets. I only got four. My favorite part was just running my hands over the bobbing cranberries.

CAROLINE

"HEY!" A cranberry bounced off Rae's head and plopped into the water. She spun around. Oliver and Tate were across the bog, smirking. Who'd thrown it? If it was Tate, she'd shrug it off, but if it was Oliver . . . well, maybe she'd get mad.

"DO NOT THROW THE CRANBERRIES!" Chef Nancy pointed her finger.

Tate and Oliver instantly tried to look busy. Rae watched them and smiled. Having them here was fun, but still, when they got back to the competition, it'd be different. They'd have to go.

····

After the bog, there was a tasting party in the large metal building. There was cranberry juice, dried cranberries, and fresh cranberries.

Caroline took a bite of a fresh red cranberry. "Agh!" She spit it out, then wiped her tongue on her sleeve. "Sorry!" Her face turned a cranberry shade of red.

Ben laughed. "No worries. Fresh cranberries are astringent: sour and bitter. But just add a little sugar and . . ." He handed her a glass of cranberry juice.

Caroline gulped it down, desperate to get rid of the nasty flavor. She nodded. "So much better."

OLIVER

The tour was a good way to get back into the group, but things definitely feel different. Especially on the way home. Tate and I sat in the back of the van and Caroline and Rae hardly even talked to us. Not that I cared—it was good to have the extra time to think of cranberry recipes. Whatever we're going to be making, I want to be prepared.

CHAPTER 10

bout time!" Steve rushed to the van as soon as it pulled into the Porter Lodge parking lot. "Chef Gary and Chef Aimee are waiting."

Steve led the group, shouting orders all the way to the filming studio. "Now go to the front. Behind the table. Face the judges. Side by side."

Rae rolled her eyes. "Like we haven't done this a million times before."

Caroline nodded. "I know."

"ROLLING."

"Welcome back from your field trip." Chef Gary surveyed the group. "This is an important challenge. We could end up with two, or maybe even three contestants for the final run to the finish line. I know you're all anxious to get started, so let's do it. Cranberries!" He held up a fresh red cranberry. "Many people only eat these once a year, and that special occasion is . . ." He raised his eyebrows.

"Thanksgiving!"

"Right. So, in the spirit of that very special day, your challenge is to create an innovative cranberry sauce. You'll have a total of eighteen minutes for this challenge. Five minutes in the pantry and thirteen minutes to prepare the sauce. We're going to start the pantry run right here, right now. Are you ready?"

"YES, CHEF!"

He raised his hand. "Your time in the pantry starts . . . NOW!"

"What to make? What to make?" Rae ran to the pantry, trying to decide. She'd had all sorts of ideas on the way back from the field trip, but now she had to pick one. She grabbed the red wine vinegar and dropped it into her basket. Decision made!

The cameras followed the junior chefs. They filmed Oliver grabbing fennel and onions, Tate picking up brown sugar and oranges, and Caroline choosing spices. Their last shot was of Rae running back to get soy sauce.

"TIME."

The junior chefs raced back to their workstations.

"LET'S GET COOKING!"

Rae unpacked her basket and looked around—no one was rushing. This challenge was easy—too easy. Anybody could make cranberry sauce. That meant one thing: a twist or trick was right around the corner. She added chili sauce, soy sauce, red wine vinegar, and red peppers to her pot, stirred it together, and dropped in the cranberries. Ten minutes later they were popping, releasing their tasty juices into the sauce. Three minutes after that, it was all over.

"TIME!"

Eight hands rose into the air. When time was called, the junior chefs had to drop everything and hold up their hands—even if they weren't finished.

Rae snuck a peek at Oliver. Here to stay or gone for good? And what about . . .

Chef Gary's voice interrupted her thoughts. "Please, bring your sauces up front. There are four numbers on the table. Set your bowl down on one of the numbers."

A shiver ran down Caroline's spine. It wasn't over!

"Knew it!" Rae set her bowl down on number four.

Chef Aimee held up a red bag. "You'll each pick a number from this bag and then go stand behind the dish on that number. If you pick your own number, you will choose again. Let's get started."

> I should have known the judges would do something sneaky. I forgot to expect the unexpected. I got number three. That's Oliver's cranberry sauce. It's pretty basic: fennel, onion, thyme, olive oil, and cranberries. Mine was much more flavorful and interesting.

CAROLINE

Rae had Tate's sauce with its flavors of brown sugar and orange rind; Oliver had Rae's sauce with its soy sauce and red peppers; and Tate had Caroline's sauce with its bold accents of ginger and cumin.

THUMP! Chef Gary banged his hand on the table. "This challenge—as you may have guessed—is not yet over. That was just part one. Are you ready for part two?"

"YES, CHEF!"

"For the second part of this challenge, you'll have forty-five minutes to create an innovative appetizer using the cranberry sauce in front of you. You'll have five minutes to plan, five minutes in the pantry, and thirty-five minutes of cooking time. Ready?"

"YES, CHEF."

"CUT."

....

Rae carried Tate's sauce back to her workstation. She took a spoon and tasted it: spicy, tangy, and sweet. There were five minutes to decide what to make.

Caroline tasted Oliver's sauce twice to be sure. Had he lost his touch? She could make whatever she wanted; his dull flavors weren't going to make a difference.

Tate started on a list of ingredients. He was going to make good into great and he already had an idea: fish cakes with a spicy apple cranberry relish. He'd thought of it instantly.

OLIVER

I'm lucky we got this redo. I missed picking up two of my ingredients, ginger and serrano peppers, in the first pantry run, so it wasn't my best effort. This is going to be different. I have a solid idea, and Rae's cranberry sauce is going to work perfectly. I'm going to incorporate Rae's sauce into the actual appetizer. I'm making glazed cranberry meatballs.

CHAPTER 11

hef Nancy visited the junior chefs before the pantry run.

Rae had a question about spring roll wraps.

"Make sure your oil is heated to three hundred and twenty-five degrees before placing the rolls in the pan."

Tate had a question about fish.

"Both haddock and cod are good choices."

Caroline had a question about walnuts.

"Pre-toasting them is an excellent idea for a pie crust."

Oliver didn't want to talk. "Thank you, Chef Nancy, but I've got this under control." Chef Nancy moved to the side of the studio.

"ROLLING!"

A minute later, the cameras were following the junior chefs into the pantry again. They zoomed in for a close-up of Oliver's hand reaching for fresh ginger, Rae picking out mushrooms, Caroline choosing Gorgonzola, and Tate's feet moving faster than anyone had seen them move before.

"TIME!"

Rae smiled as she unpacked her basket and waited for the signal to start. This was more like it. The room was filled with energy.

"LET'S GET COOKING!"

Caroline grabbed a large frying pan, dumped in a single layer of walnuts, and turned on the heat. In five minutes, those walnuts would be toasty brown. She pulled out the food processor and started on the pie crust. If she was going to be finished in thirty-five minutes, she couldn't do one thing at a time—it had to be double-duty.

Tate rinsed the haddock fillet, patted it dry with a paper towel, sliced it into quarters, wrapped it in foil, and put it

into the oven. Small pieces cooked faster, and he needed all the speed he could get. He grabbed two potatoes, quartered them, put them into a pot of water, and turned on the burner. Next, he got to work on his relish. Once everything was cooking, he'd feel better. The clock was not going to be his friend.

Chef Gary arrived just as he was dicing apples. "Wow, good knife skills."

"Thank you, Chef. I'm working on a relish." He grabbed a knob of ginger, peeled it, and then expertly began mincing.

"Keep it up!"

Rae was doing double-duty too, frying chicken and trying to chop vegetables at the same time.

She stopped when she saw Chef Gary. "Normally I'd bake the chicken in the oven, but there isn't time, so I'm frying it. It's faster." She picked up a stalk of celery and started chopping.

Chef Gary pointed to the frying pan. "You might want to check on that."

Rae grabbed a spatula and flipped the chicken over. A minute more and it might have burned.

OLIVER

Chef Gary came to visit me right when I was mixing up the ingredients for my meatballs. Everyone else was running around like chickens with their heads cut off, but not me. I was calm and confident. Chef Gary noticed right away. My dish takes thirty-five minutes to make. I'm not trying to stuff fifty minutes of prep time into a thirty-five-minute time slot. I'm respectful of food and time.

Chef Gary closed his eyes and breathed deep. Caroline was caramelizing fennel, onion, and thyme. "I do love fennel and onions."

Caroline nodded and added balsamic vinegar to Oliver's cranberry sauce and turned off the heat.

"Almost done?"

"No." She bent down, pulled a mini pie crust from the oven, and set it on a rack to cool. Her hands were shaking. "This still has to go back into the oven once I add the filling."

"FIFTEEN MINUTES."

Caroline groaned. Would she even make it?

Chef Gary tapped the table. "Come on, Caroline, concentrate! Keep going!"

She nodded and turned back to the stove. Was there time to let the pie crust cool? No, she had to get the filling in there as soon as possible.

"TEN MINUTES."

Caroline peered into the oven, Tate dropped his fish cake into a sizzling frying pan, Rae poured oil into her wok, and Oliver stirred his meatballs in a spicy cranberry glaze.

"FIVE MINUTES!"

Chef Gary clapped his hands. "Let's get plating!"

Oliver arranged purple and green slaw in the middle of his plate, drizzled a zigzag of thinned cranberry sauce on top, and then lined up three glazed meatballs in the center. He finished by decoratively sprinkling the plate with slivers of orange peel and minced scallions.

Caroline set her mini pie on the plate. It was still hot. Hopefully she wouldn't be called first. It needed time to set. She garnished the plate with a sage leaf and whole toasted walnuts.

Rae grabbed a large romaine leaf and pushed it flat against the plate. This wasn't her first choice for plating, but it would hide the bottom of her spring rolls. They'd stuck to the pan and broken apart. She put two rolls on the leaf and stacked a third on top, then added a mini ramekin of the cranberry sriracha dipping sauce to the side and sprinkled minced parsley and pickled ginger on top.

Tate placed his fish cake in the middle of a large plate and arranged the apple cranberry relish around it like a moat. He stepped back. "Done!"

"TIME!"

Eight hands shot into the air.

"CUT!"

CHAPTER 12

Rae eyed Caroline's plate as the cameras moved in for the close-ups. It looked good. Hopefully it tasted good too. Her broken spring rolls wouldn't win, but maybe Caroline had a chance. She crossed her fingers and made a wish. *Please let Caroline win. Send Oliver and Tate home.*

Steve waved his hands. "PLACES, EVERYONE! LET'S GO!"

They rushed back to their workstations.

"ROLLING!"

Chef Gary rested his hands on the long table. "Well, that was exciting. This room was buzzing with energy."

"And everyone was busy, busy, busy," added Chef Aimee. "I can't wait to taste these creations. Let's start with . . . Caroline. Can you please bring your plate to the table and tell us what you've made?"

Caroline walked nervously to the front and set her dish

down. "I made a cranberry Gorgonzola tart with a toasted walnut crust."

"Oooh, it looks wonderful." Chef Aimee motioned for Chef Nancy to join them. She handed out forks and then started to cut into the pie. The filling oozed out onto the plate. "Goodness, is this set?" She pulled the knife out. "Caroline, is there a chance this isn't fully cooked?"

Caroline's face flushed. "Maybe, but it's mostly cooked. It probably only needed five more minutes."

Chef Gary pushed the plate to the side. "I'm sorry, Caroline. You can't expect us to eat uncooked eggs. However, on the plus side, your presentation was very nice."

"Thank you, Chef." Caroline felt sick to her stomach. But she wasn't the only one. Rae felt it too. She looked from Tate to Oliver, then back to Oliver again. Who would be staying? She crossed her fingers and made a new wish.

Tate was next. He carried his plate to the front, grinning all the way. "I made Indian-spiced fish cakes with an apple cranberry relish."

Chef Aimee stared at the plate. "Not the most innovative plating, but let's taste it."

"Mmm, nice layer of flavors."

"This sweet relish is wonderful with the fish."

"I agree." Chef Gary took another bite. "This relish is delicious. Well done, Tate. Tell us, how did you change Caroline's cranberry sauce?"

Tate shuffled uncomfortably. "I . . . uh . . . added apples."

"That's it?" Chef Gary looked confused.

"Well, I was going to add more, but there wasn't time."

"Time seems to be something of a problem in this challenge. Thank you, Tate. Let's continue. Rae, will you please bring your plate to the table."

Rae walked shakily to the front. Her lettuce wasn't going to fool the judges. She wasn't going to win, Caroline wasn't going to win, and now Tate wasn't going to win. That meant . . . She swallowed hard and set her plate on the table. "I made crispy spring rolls with a spicy sweet cranberry sauce."

"Lettuce?" Chef Aimee studied the plate, and then carefully lifted one of the rolls up with her fork. "I thought so. They stuck to the pan, didn't they?"

Rae nodded.

"That happens when your oil isn't hot enough. Were you rushed?"

Rae nodded again.

Chef Gary cut one of the spring rolls in half and dipped it into the sauce. "The chicken seems a little chewy. Poaching or baking would have been a better idea. Your flavors are nice, though. Sophisticated."

"Salty and sweet with umami undertones."

Chef Aimee tried the sauce again. "It's spicy, but the sweetness takes it down to just the right amount of heat. Was Tate's sauce spicy too?"

Oliver

"Just a little, but I added teriyaki, soy, and sriracha to deepen the flavor."

"Nicely done, Rae. We all like it."

Chef Gary smiled at Oliver. "Last but not least: Oliver, please bring your dish to the table. What have you made us?"

"I made cranberry glazed pork meatballs."

The judges were instantly filled with praise.

"Look at the color!"

"Sophisticated presentation."

"Delightful plating."

Rae wanted to cover her ears, especially once they started tasting it.

"YUM!"

"Meaty and satisfying."

"Sweet, spice, and comfort. It has everything."

Chef Gary pointed his empty fork at Oliver. "How did you change Rae's sauce?"

"I added fresh ginger, brown sugar, mustard, and some peppers to spice it up a bit. I needed something more flavorful than Rae's plain cranberry sauce to accent my pork meatballs."

"Well done, Oliver!"

Rae shot Oliver a nasty look. *Plain* cranberry sauce? How dare he! Her sauce had been sweet, spicy, *and* sophisticated!

The judges moved off to the side to decide on the winner, but no one was holding their breath. They all knew who was going to win.

OLIVER

My favorite part of winning was listening to everyone else getting lectured on what I already knew. Time! It's an important ingredient. Rushing through a recipe never ends well. They all tried to do too much in too little time. But not me. So here I am, back where I belong. And from now on, I won't make *any* mistakes.

••••

That night, after saying goodbye to a teary-eyed Tate, Caroline and Rae were back in their room, in pajamas, in their beds.

"I can't believe he's back!"

"And here to stay!"

"I thought we were done with him!"

"Me too."

"It's the worst!" Caroline pulled the covers over her head. "I'll probably have nightmares."

Rae stared at the lump in Caroline's bed. Was it really the worst? Wasn't one against one worse? Together against Oliver had to be better. *Together! The opposite of alone.*

CHAPTER 13

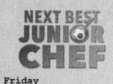

CONFIDENTIAL!
Schedule of Events for
Week Three
(Episode Three)

Friday
  ???
Saturday
  Field trip!
  Challenge
Sunday
  Challenge
Monday
  Lesson
  Mini-challenge
  Challenge

Tuesday
  Challenge
Wednesday
  Field trip!
  Challenge
Thursday
  Final winner-take-all
    challenge

hef Nancy was waiting at the breakfast table. She waved the schedules for the week. "Grab some breakfast and I'll hand these out."

Caroline walked straight to the sugared cereal. "After yesterday, I can't afford to take chances."

Rae picked an apple fritter.

Oliver sat down across from her with a glass of orange juice, two muffins, and a chocolate croissant. "Breakfast of champions!"

She ignored him.

Caroline scanned the schedule. "With Friday and Saturday down, only five challenges left, not including the final challenge on Thursday."

Rae shook her head. "There could be even *more* surprises." She looked up at Chef Nancy for clues, but her face was blank.

Oliver raised his hand. "Is there a Golden Envelope again like last week?" In week two, the Golden Envelope had given Oliver an advantage. Another shot at an advantage would be invaluable and get him even closer to winning it all.

Chef Nancy's phone buzzed. "I'm sorry, I've got to take this. We'll do interviews in thirty minutes and then head out to the challenge. All will be explained. Enjoy your breakfast."

Caroline tapped the paper. "There's another field trip on—"

"I'm not doing any kind of pact!" interrupted Oliver. "This is our last week and I'm here to win. Just so you know." He bit into his croissant and smiled.

I'm the odd guy out and I like that. It gives me power. My being here is putting Caroline and Rae on edge. It's me against them. At this point, I don't think either of them is much of a threat. They have each other, so it won't be so bad when they lose. They can be together.

OLIVER

RAE

Oliver is such a boaster. I don't know how he can come in here and just take over. He's not even supposed to be here. Caroline and I have to shut him down, and fast. We can do it. He underestimates us, and that's an advantage.

Oliver doesn't make things easier. He should try to be less prickly. I don't know what else to say. I'm not going to say bad things about him to the world. I'm just not that kind of person. I will win or Rae will win. I'd be really happy with either of those outcomes.

CAROLINE

When Chef Nancy came back, Oliver, Rae, and Caroline were ready and waiting at the door.

····

It was a short golf cart ride to the back meadow behind Porter Lodge. Chef Nancy stopped on the hill overlooking the field below.

"It's a party!" said Oliver.

"With kids!" Rae pointed right. "There's a round bouncy thing. It kind of looks like a donut."

"And a white tent for us." Caroline pointed left.

"Seems about right!" Chef Nancy powered the cart forward. "Let's go see."

Steve was waiting with the camerapeople and the judges. He jumped into action.

"ROLLING!"

Chef Nancy handed everyone their aprons and a minute later they were lined up in front of *all* the judges.

Chef Gary waved a shiny gold envelope. "Welcome! Does this look familiar?"

"YES, CHEF!"

"You bet it does. This is the Golden Envelope. And inside is an advantage for the winner-take-all round on Thursday.

Now, the important question you're asking yourself is *How can I win it?* What do you think, Chef Aimee? Should we tell them? How can they win it?"

"With this!" Chef Aimee held up a small enamel pin shaped like a mixing whisk. "As you've probably noticed, we are no longer using the Gadget Wall or stars on the black board. Instead, we are giving out pins every time you win a challenge. On Thursday morning, the apron with the most whisk pins will win the Golden Envelope. Excited?"

"YES, CHEF!"

"Glad to hear it. Oliver and Rae, will you please come forward? You have each won a challenge this week." She pinned a whisk pin on their aprons. Everyone applauded.

Chef Gary pointed to the bouncy thing in the distance. "Kids are bouncing. What does it remind you of?"

Oliver's hand shot into the air. "Donut!"

Rae glared at him. That was her guess! He'd stolen it.

"Very good, Oliver! This is a donut challenge! You'll have ninety minutes to make two dozen donuts. One dozen to be judged by the bouncing kids, so make them kid-friendly, and the other dozen to be judged by . . ."

Chef Porter stepped forward. "A more sophisticated palate. I have to confess, I do like a good donut!"

Chef Aimee nodded. "Me too! The three of us will be judging your fancy donut. The scores for both the kid donut and the fancy donut will be added together to determine one winner for this challenge." She pointed to the big white tent. "You'll have five minutes to plan, five minutes in the pantry, and then ninety minutes to cook. Due to time constraints, you will be provided with the same premade donut dough, but it will be up to you to select the correct rising time and cooking temperature. Remember, we want to see some innovative thinking. Are you ready?"

"YES, CHEF!"

Chef Gary waved his arm. "Great! Let's go inside the tent!"

CHAPTER 14

I'm really excited about this challenge. I've never made donuts before, but I have made beignets. That's a French dessert that's kind of like a mini donut, so I'm not nervous. My lucky charm is cereal, so my kid donut will have a cereal-infused glaze and maybe even a filling. I'm still deciding on that.

CAROLINE

Rae hastily scribbled down notes. She was making a banana cream filling for the fancy donut, but the kid donut was the challenge. What could she do that was different?

Oliver added two final ingredients to his list, then put down his pen. He was ready.

The pantry run was fast and easy, and everyone came back with at least four jars of sprinkles.

Chef Nancy delivered the dough. Everyone got two large cloth-covered bowls and the same instructions. "Roll out your dough. Cut out your donuts. Let them rise, then fry."

"ROLLING."

"LET'S GET COOKING!"

Rae rolled out her dough until it was half an inch thick. She picked out two cookie cutters, one for the outside and one for the donut holes. Half would have holes, the others filling. She covered the shapes with a cloth and put them on the side to rise.

RAE

My kid donut has to look special and different. Everyone is going to use sprinkles, so I have to do something above and beyond to stand out. I think I have a really good idea: a unicorn donut! I'm going to use donut holes stacked on a stick to make the horn. The donut will be the face it rests on once I decorate it. It'll be a lot of work, but that's what you have to do to win.

Oliver had a plan: prepare everything, and then assemble. First up, salted caramel. He set a saucepan on the heat, added one-quarter cup of water and one cup of sugar, then turned on the oven. Candied pecans would be next.

Chef Aimee visited the junior chefs to check on their

progress. Caroline was making cereal milk, Rae was mashing bananas, and Oliver was melting marshmallows in a mixture of sugar, butter, vanilla, and salt.

She lifted the edge of the cloth to look at his donuts. "Are they ready to fry?"

Oliver touched the dough with his finger. "The dough is springing back too fast. When it springs back more slowly, then it'll be ready." He leaned forward and whispered. "Probably just ten more minutes."

Chef Aimee put a finger to her lips. "Secret's safe with me."

"THIRTY MINUTES."

Oliver checked his donuts and then turned on the burner. There was an art to frying—you have to work in small batches and not overcrowd the pot. Too many donuts and the temperature would drop. He looked at the thermometer and waited. Three hundred and sixty-five degrees was his magic number.

Caroline dropped three donuts into the hot oil and waited. They sank to the bottom of the pan and then slowly rose to the surface. Two minutes per side and then they were done. She pulled them out of the oil and set them on a stack of paper towels to drain. Paper towels pulled the grease out.

Rae looked at the clock. Time was running out. In between batches, she'd have to wait for the oil temperature to rise before she could start again. She looked around and felt better. They were all stuck doing the same thing. The first thirty minutes had been crucial, and she'd used her time wisely. She'd made pink lemonade icing, vanilla icing, caramelized banana pudding, a mango glaze, and a dark chocolate ganache. She dropped a handful of donut holes into the hot oil. Once they were done, she'd turn them into unicorn horns.

Twenty minutes isn't a lot of time to decorate two dozen donuts, but my *mise en place* makes me incredibly efficient. Having everything prepared and in its place is a real time-saver.

OLIVER

Oliver gave Chef Gary a demonstration. "It's a four-step process. Dunk in salted caramel sauce, dip in toasted coconut, drizzle on dark chocolate hazelnut sauce, and then sprinkle on candied pecans." Oliver set the finished donut on a tray.

Chef Gary licked his lips. "Are those extras?" He pointed to a tray of fried donut holes.

"No, sir, I might still use them."

Chef Gary nodded and forced himself to step back.

Caroline had a system too. "I do one big dip and two mini dips. The big dip coats the whole top in icing, and then I do a mini dip for cereal and a mini dip for sprinkles." She held up a finished donut. It was half-covered in colorful cereal pieces and half-covered in rainbow sprinkles.

"What happened to you?" Chef Gary almost gasped when he saw Rae. She was covered in pastry cream.

"Pudding explosion!" She held up the piping bag. "These things aren't easy to use. But it's okay. I only have one more." She picked up a donut, poked the end with a chopstick to make a hole, and then inserted the tip of the piping bag. One squeeze and she was done.

Chef Gary sniffed the air. "Is that banana?"

"Caramelized banana! With mango glaze and—"

"Stop!" Chef Gary raised his hands and turned away. "This is torture!"

CHAPTER 15

ae glanced at the clock. Fifteen minutes left! She took a deep breath. One step at a time—that was the only way to get things done. She filled the pastry bags: one with chocolate and the other with pink, then got to work. Each unicorn donut had two dark ganache slits for eyes, four eyelashes each, and a circle of pink icing around the horn. That was a lot of piping detail! But if she was fast, she could make it.

"TEN MINUTES!"

Oliver studied his tray of donuts. They had marshmallow icing, chocolate drizzles, and sprinkles, but was that enough? What did kids *really* like? Kids liked more! He picked up a donut hole, dipped it in icing, rolled it in chocolate sprinkles, and stuck it in the middle of the donut. There. More!

Caroline spread the sweet cream cheese icing over the edge of the donut so it dripped down the sides in swirly waves. She filled a piping bag with the spicy strawberry glaze and outlined three petals on each side of the donut hole. Was it a winning combination? Hopefully.

"FIVE MINUTES!"

Rae hit the mix button. Banana chips, dried mango, and sugar swirled together. She emptied the banana mango sugar into a bowl, but it was too late—the smooth mango glaze on the top of her donuts was set. There was no way the sugared topping would stick. She wet a paper towel with hot water, dabbed the top of a donut, and then quickly sprinkled the sugar over the imperfection. Would it stay? Would it cover it up? There wasn't time for crossed fingers. She had eleven more to go.

"TIME!"

Six hands went up.

"CUT!"

CRASH!

A bowl hit the floor.

"Sorry." Rae bent down to pick it up. There was sugar everywhere—on her, and all over the floor.

Chef Nancy rushed over. "Oh dear, you're a mess. It's okay." She handed Rae a new apron. "And don't forget to switch your pin!"

Rae nodded. She *wasn't* going to forget that.

"Junior chefs!" Steve waved from the front of the room. "Please bring your fancy donuts to the table and stand behind your trays."

Rae watched the judges file in and take their places. They'd all done this a dozen times, but it was still exciting.

"ROLLING!"

Chef Gary licked his lips. "Finally! We get to taste these, and if they taste as good as they look, it's going to be a hard decision." He turned to Chef Aimee. "We might have to eat more than one to decide."

"You'd like that, wouldn't you."

He put his hand over his heart. "I'd do it for the show and—"

"Chef Gary!" Chef Porter winked at the contestants. "Do you want to talk or taste?"

"Good point!" He turned back to the table. "Let's get started. Caroline, can you tell us what you've made?"

"My donut has a sweet cream cheese icing and is complemented by a peppered strawberry glaze."

"Charming design!"

"Nicely executed."

"Sophisticated."

"Pretty." Chef Gary picked one up and took a bite. "MMM! Tasty, too." He took another bite. "Sweet and spicy." He popped the last bit into his mouth. "And perfectly fluffy."

The other chefs were equally impressed, and Chef Porter liked it so much, she had two bites.

Caroline looked down the table—going first had its advantages. Would they still be hungry when they got to Oliver's donut? Maybe not.

Chef Aimee pointed to Rae's tray. "Rae, can you tell us what you've made?"

"My donut has a caramelized banana cream filling and is frosted with mango glaze and accented with banana mango sugar."

Chef Porter moved up for a closer look. "A filled donut? In our short time span? That's impressive. And what exactly is banana mango sugar?"

"Banana chips mixed with sugar and dried mango pieces . . . in the food processor."

Chef Porter picked up a donut and a napkin. She nibbled, swallowed, and then took a bigger bite. A drop of banana pudding dripped onto her chin.

Napkin, thought Rae. But instead, Chef Porter licked it with her tongue.

Chef Aimee loved the mix of mango and banana, and Chef Gary ate his in two bites.

"Oliver!" Chef Gary hungrily eyed the tray of donuts. "Can you tell us what you've made?"

"Yes, Chef. I made a salted caramel glazed donut with a dark chocolate hazelnut drizzle. It's accented by toasted coconut shavings and candied pecans."

Chef Gary reached forward. "I've been waiting to try this ever since I first saw it. It looks delicious."

Oliver smirked. Rae and Caroline tried not to look worried.

Chef Gary bit deep into the donut. "The texture and the taste are good . . . but the topping seems a little heavy for such a light, fluffy donut. It's delicious, but maybe more suited to a cake donut. Something that can handle the richness."

Chef Aimee took a bite. "I see what you mean. There needs to be more mass, more donut, but I do like the flavors."

Chef Porter wiped her mouth with the napkin. "Salty sweet is such a nice combination, but this topping is a little heavy-handed. Less might have been more."

Caroline wondered, *Did anyone else notice?* Oliver's donut was the only one Chef Gary didn't finish.

"CUT."

CHAPTER 16

Caroline watched Steve the producer. His arms were in the air and he was shouting, again. "Bring your kid donut trays up here for the judges. After we film this segment, we'll take them outside to the kids. Stand behind your tray and when we get to you, give us a description of your donut."

I made a cereal-infused glaze for my donut and decorated it with sprinkles and crumbled sweet cereal.

CAROLINE

OLIVER

I made a marshmallow glaze and covered it with sprinkles, then added on a bonus chocolate-sprinkled donut hole.

I made a unicorn donut decorated with nonpareils. The glaze is flavored with pink lemonade, and the horn is iced donut holes.

RAE

"CUT!"

Steve waved his hand and helpers picked up the trays and took them out the back door. The judges followed.

Chef Nancy caught Caroline's look of concern. "Don't worry—it's for the judging."

"I know." Caroline forced a smile, but after seeing Rae's donut, she was pretty sure she didn't have a chance. A unicorn donut—*that* was genius!

OLIVER

Just because a donut looks like a unicorn doesn't mean it tastes good. And don't kids prefer chocolate?

It wasn't easy to wait and do nothing. Chef Nancy pointed to the trays of fancy donuts. "The judges said you could try them. Don't be shy. I'm not—I'll try them too."

Caroline nudged Rae. "I'll try yours if you try mine."

"Deal." Rae picked up one of Caroline's donuts and took a bite. "Oh, Caroline! This is really good! And your donut is fluffier than mine."

Caroline nodded and blushed. She would have said more, but her mouth was full of creamy banana goodness.

"This!" Caroline held up her half-eaten donut. "Is so good it should be illegal."

"Mmm, mmm, mmm," agreed Chef Nancy. A drop of banana cream dripped onto her shirt.

Oliver couldn't watch. He turned and looked at the floor. So what if he didn't win this one. It was a good lesson: Less is more. It sounded familiar. Had he heard that before?

····

Ten minutes later, Steve was back with cameras, the judges, and a little girl. "Junior chefs, line up in front of the judges.

"ROLLING!"

Chef Porter moved to the center. "Welcome back. We

have deliberated amongst ourselves, and we have tallied the votes of the children." Chef Porter pointed to the little girl. "Annabelle is our special guest today, and she has in her hand the name of the winning kid donut. Annabelle, will you please read the card."

Annabelle took a giant step forward and shouted, "UNICORN DONUT!" She looked up at Chef Porter. "It was my favorite too, but not because of the unicorn. I like butterflies better, because they're real . . . and pretty. But I like pink lemonade . . . and frosting. And lots of big chocolate sprinkles." She stepped back into line, nodding.

"Well, you heard it here!" Chef Aimee suppressed a laugh. "Thank you, Annabelle."

Annabelle looked like she might have more to say, but Chef Nancy quickly gave her the *shush* sign: a finger to the lips.

Chef Aimee watched to see if it would work, and then, satisfied, she continued. "As for the fancy donut, the judges' vote was unanimous. Rae, you are the winner. Your donut was inventive and original, and the creamy filling was just the right amount of decadent. Well done! Please come to the front." Everyone clapped.

Chef Aimee pinned a whisk pin onto Rae's apron. The two pins sparkled under the camera lights. "Congratulations! But there's one more thing, something fun." She winked at Rae. "Almost everyone likes it. Any ideas?"

Rae took a guess. "The fate of Chef Gary?" Each week, the junior chefs had been given an opportunity to have fun with Chef Gary. In week one, it was the dunk tank filled with green Jell-O. In week two, it was a roller-skating sundae-making obstacle course. What would it be this week?

"Absolutely! And today your choices are Roly Poly or Topsy Turvey!"

"ROLY POLY!"

"ROLY POLY!"

"Roly Poly!" decided Rae.

"Nooooo." Chef Gary waved his hands. "Not that one!"

CHAPTER 17

The field outside was covered in large red foam tubes that stood almost seven feet tall. An assistant rolled an enormous yellow ball toward Chef Aimee. It was bigger than Chef Gary.

Chef Aimee tapped the ball. "Have you ever seen a gerbil in a ball? Well, this is kind of the same, only Chef Gary is the gerbil."

Caroline looked at Chef Gary, then the ball, and then burst out laughing.

Chef Gary puffed out his chest. "I'm not scared." He pointed at the junior chefs. "And don't think you're just going to stand there and watch. We're in this together."

"Absolutely." Chef Aimee nodded. "This is a team effort. Once Chef Gary's in the ball, it's up to you to help him knock down those tubes—like he's the bowling ball. If Chef Gary can knock over twenty tubes in five minutes, a donation of twenty thousand dollars will be made to Kanter's Camp

Kitchen. This is a camp that provides culinary instruction, free of charge, for children between the ages of seven and fourteen. What do you think? Is that a good cause?"

"YES, CHEF!"

Rae raised her hand. "But how do we help?"

Chef Aimee nudged the ball. "You can push the ball, tell him which way to go, and offer words of encouragement. Chef Gary needs you, because once he's inside, he can't see out."

"Nothing at all?" asked Rae.

Chef Aimee shook her head. "Nothing."

Caroline looked over the field. There were a lot of tubes, maybe a hundred, but they weren't close together. Maybe this wasn't going to be so easy.

The assistant inserted a small hose into the ball and started a motor. "This keeps air in the ball while I open the door." He pulled down on a zipper. Chef Gary stepped inside; the assistant zipped the door closed and took the hose away.

Rae strained her eyes. "I can't see him in there!"

Chef Aimee pushed the ball. "Chef Gary, are you ready?"

There was a muffled "Yes."

She looked at the junior chefs. "Are you ready?"

"YES, CHEF!"

She raised her hand and looked at her stopwatch. "GO!"

Oliver pushed left, Caroline yelled "RIGHT," Rae yelled "STRAIGHT," and the ball took off to the left.

"NO! NO! STOP!"

They chased after it.

Oliver knocked on the ball. "Chef Gary, don't move, sir. We need a plan." He paused for a moment, thinking, then . . . "How about a guide? Someone out front planning where to go next?"

Rae nodded. "And the two other people can help move the ball."

"I'll be the guide!" Caroline ran ahead. "Follow me!"

Rae tapped the ball. "STRAIGHT AHEAD, CHEF GARY!"

"A LITTLE LEFT!" yelled Oliver.

A tube fell to the ground.

"WE GOT IT! YAY!" Caroline ran to the right. "THIS ONE'S NEXT!"

Six tubes later, they had a system—if Chef Gary got a little off-track, they just pushed him back into place.

Chef Gary was fast. Oliver and Rae were panting to keep up. Sometimes he was too fast, like the time he fell down in the ball. No one could see it, but the ball suddenly stopped and there was a loud yelp.

"TWO AND A HALF MINUTES!" yelled Chef Aimee.

"SEVEN MORE!" yelled Caroline.

Rae jogged next to Oliver. "Can we do it? Seven more tubes."

"RIGHT!" yelled Oliver. He shoved the ball. "WE CAN DO IT!"

"SIX TO GO!" Caroline took off to the left. "THIS ONE'S CLOSE!"

"LEFT!" Rae shouted, and the ball knocked over another tube.

With twenty-six seconds left, tube number twenty hit the ground.

"WE DID IT!" Caroline threw her arms in the air.

The assistant came running, followed by Chef Aimee and Chef Nancy. He unzipped the ball. Chef Gary crawled out, tried to stand up, then sat down. "Too dizzy!" He was covered in sweat.

"Goodness!" Chef Aimee kneeled down. "Are you okay?" She handed him a water bottle.

He emptied it in one gulp and then slowly got to his feet. "We did it!" He weakly raised his arm.

"YAY, CHEF GARY!"

CHAPTER 18

R ae walked to the breakfast table smiling. Yesterday had changed things. She felt better about Oliver.

Caroline filled a bowl with cereal. "I'm ready for lessons and more challenges." This was her chance to catch up and finally get a whisk pin.

"I kind of like lessons," said Oliver.

"I heard about that." Rae quickly covered her mouth. "Oops, sorry." Caroline had told her about how Oliver had taken professional cooking lessons.

Oliver shrugged. No big deal—nothing was going to bother him. There were two challenges today, and tonight he'd have three pins. He couldn't wait to get started.

CAROLINE

It was like old times. We joked and laughed all the way to the school studio. It's hard to be mad at Oliver anymore. It feels like he belongs.

....

Chef Nancy walked to the fridge and came back with a dozen eggs. "With all the sophisticated skills and techniques you've mastered in the past two weeks, it's still important to remember the basics." She held up an egg. "Can anyone tell me the characteristics of a perfect hard-boiled egg?"

"Firm yellow."

"No green ring around the yellow."

"Tender white and not rubbery."

Chef Nancy put four eggs in the bottom of a saucepan and covered them with an inch of water. "You never want to boil your eggs." She put the saucepan on the burner. "But you do want to boil your water. As soon as it boils, turn it down to a low simmer and cover. Leave for ten to eleven minutes, then pull your eggs out and drop them into a bowl of ice water. Anyone know why?"

Caroline raised her hand. "To stop the cooking."

"Exactly." Chef Nancy reached under the counter and brought up a bowl of peeled hard-boiled eggs. "The added bonus is that it also makes them easier to peel." She sliced one open. "See how the yolk is bright yellow and firm. There's beauty in a perfectly cooked egg." She sliced the remaining four eggs and put the yolks in a bowl. "What is a deviled egg?"

"A bad egg!" joked Rae.

Caroline laughed.

Chef Nancy held up a fork. "Maybe, but it's also a delicious egg." She mashed the yolks, then mixed in mustard, mayonnaise, salt, and pepper. When the texture was smooth and creamy, she filled a piping bag and then piped the filling back into the cup of each egg white. "And now the finishing touch!" She sprinkled paprika on top and then passed the platter. "Try one. I want you to notice the taste and the texture. They work together to enrich the experience."

Caroline reached for one. "I like deviled eggs!"

Rae and Oliver agreed.

Something caught the corner of Caroline's eye. She turned. "The cameras are here!"

"Mini-challenge," whispered Rae.

"I'm ready!" said Oliver, and he popped another egg in his mouth.

Chef Nancy waited for the signal from the producer. "Your challenge is to create an inventive deviled egg. You have a total of twenty-five minutes to pick out ingredients from the pantry and make six samples of your egg. Let's get cooking!"

Oliver was in and out of the pantry in two minutes. He wanted his eggs on the stove and cooking as soon as possible. He looked at the clock. That gave him almost ten minutes to prepare everything else, and then a few minutes for plating. Once the eggs were done, he'd be rushing, but for now he had time. He sliced a shallot into thin, small rings and dropped them into a sizzling pan of oil. When they were crispy golden brown, he scooped them out and put them on a paper towel to drain. He checked the timer: four minutes left on the eggs.

Caroline preheated her oven to four hundred degrees, then put two pots of eggs on the stove. She placed a thin slice of prosciutto on a baking sheet between two pieces of parchment paper and then added a weighted pie plate on top. Ham curled as it cooked, but not this time—it was going to stay flat.

Making candied jalapeños was simple, but dangerous. Rae pulled on a pair of protective gloves. Jalapeño juice on a finger could get in an eye, and then it would be painful times a hundred. She sliced the jalapeño and added it to the simmering mixture of vinegar, sugar, and lime juice on the stove.

Once the jalapeños were cooked she'd pull them out, reduce the liquid, then add them back again.

••••

The last five minutes were busy but satisfying. Everyone liked plating.

Caroline scooped her yellow yolk mix into the piping bag and then carefully filled each egg white cup. Some of the eggs had been hard to peel, but she'd made extras, and these six on the plate were perfect. She scattered seasoned breadcrumbs on top, sprinkled on thinly sliced chives, and added an upright ham chip as the finishing touch.

Rae added a sprig of cilantro and one pickled jalapeño to the top of each of her eggs.

Oliver carefully arranged the crispy shallots on top of his eggs. Then he stepped back, crossed his arms, and waited for Chef Nancy to call time.

"TIME!"

CHAPTER 19

When the cameras were done filming the eggs, the junior chefs moved their plates to the big table.

Chef Nancy pointed to the door. "Here comes our surprise guest."

Chef Porter walked through the door. "Good morning, everyone!"

"Good morning, Chef."

She studied the table. "Well, these all look wonderful. Junior chefs, can you tell us what you've made?"

My inspiration was eggs Benedict. I made deviled eggs with seasoned breadcrumbs and baked prosciutto chips.

CAROLINE

OLIVER

I made smoky deviled eggs with sun-dried tomatoes and a crispy shallot topping.

I made guacamole deviled eggs with a candied jalapeño garnish.

RAE

Chef Nancy handed Chef Porter a napkin. "You pick first."

"Mmmm!" Chef Porter made the same sound for every egg. It was impossible to tell which she liked the best. Chef Porter and Chef Nancy went to the back of the room to choose a winner.

Caroline watched them closely, looking for clues, but there weren't any. Normally when the judges returned they were smiling, but not this time. They looked serious.

Chef Nancy shook her head. "This wasn't easy. We loved all of your interesting flavors and creative presentations."

Chef Porter raised a finger ". . . But there was one point of difference. Caroline, your eggs were perfectly cooked *and* peeled—not one single blemish." She looked at Rae and Oliver. "You had a little trouble with the peeling, didn't you?"

They nodded.

Chef Porter pulled a pin out of her pocket. "And your prosciutto chip—that was a standout. Congratulations, Caroline. You are the winner of this challenge. Please come to the front and accept your pin."

Oliver clapped with everyone else. The day wasn't over yet. As long as he got that other pin to be even with Rae, he could live with that.

I'm so glad I made extra eggs. That's a good tip for the future. Make more than you need. I love my pin! It makes me feel like I can do anything!

CAROLINE

CHAPTER 20

"SURPRISE!" Chef Aimee burst through the door. "I'm here to help Chef Nancy on this next really *cool* challenge."

Chef Nancy surveyed the group. "Shall we get started? Chef Aimee is right. This *is* a cool challenge, and it's fun, too. There's no lesson, so we'll jump right in." She motioned to Steve.

He nodded. "ROLLING."

"This is the icebox cake challenge! So, let me ask: What is an icebox?"

Rae raised her hand. "It's an old-fashioned name for a refrigerator."

"Exactly. So I guess you could say this is . . . an old-fashioned challenge. Icebox cakes were popular in the 1950s and recently have had a resurgence in popularity. Do you know why?" Chef Nancy held up three fingers. "No baking, they're fun to make, *and* they're delicious! Your challenge now is to create a no-bake icebox cake, which is basically cookies layered with whipped cream or other creamy filling." She bent down and picked up a round springform pan. "There are two important limitations to this challenge. You must prepare your cake in this pan, and you may not use the oven. The stovetop can be used to create your fillings, and you may use cookies and crackers for your cake layers. The pantry will be open for the duration of this challenge. You'll have twenty minutes to assemble your cake, and then we'll put them in the refrigerator to set. Chef Aimee and I will return with you here after dinner for the judging."

Rae smiled. Chef Nancy was right. This *did* sound like fun.

"Are you ready?"

"YES, CHEF!"

"Let's get cooking!"

OLIVER

I'm going to make a multilayered lime cake with a fresh strawberry filling. *Cold, fruit, fresh*—those are my inspiration words. I'll make as many layers as I can, so I'll be looking for super-thin wafer cookies in the pantry.

My first idea is usually my best idea. Bavarian apple pie—that's my inspiration. Apples, graham crackers, and cream cheese—maybe walnuts for decoration, too.

RAE

CAROLINE

I haven't done anything with chocolate yet, so this is going to be new for the judges. I'm going to use chocolate wafers and hot chocolate mixed with whipping cream for my filling. Hot chocolate icebox cake: It's going to be as good as it sounds.

Rae had a plan. Make the fillings and the frosting and then, when everything was ready, assemble the cake. Caroline and Oliver had the exact same plan. Rae peeled and sliced four apples and put them in a frying pan with butter and sugar. She added a squeeze of lemon juice for flavor and stability.

Chef Aimee looked over the group and smiled. Not only were they busy, but at this exact moment they were all stirring the very same ingredient: whipping cream. Rae folded it into her cream cheese filling, Caroline whisked it vigorously, and Oliver added vanilla and sugar to make it sweet.

Oliver dipped a spoon into his lime filling and then tasted it. Evaporated milk, condensed milk, and lime juice—only three ingredients, but it was delicious. Simple was better. He covered the bottom of the pan with filling, then added a layer of thin wafers, a layer of fresh strawberry compote and whipped cream, then another layer of wafers. He repeated the process until it reached the top of the pan.

Caroline and Rae were adding layers too. Caroline added chocolate wafers, caramel sauce, hot chocolate whipped cream, and then wafers again. She was hoping to get five repeats before the top of the pan.

Rae was not so lucky. She'd cut her apples too thick. She'd be lucky to get three full layers. Maybe first ideas weren't so good after all.

"TIME!"

Six hands rose into the air.

Chef Nancy pointed to the pantry. "Into the refrigerator and then back to the lodge!"

CHAPTER 21

aroline and Oliver were chatty all the way back to the lodge. They were both thinking the same thing: two hours from now they'd have a new whisk pin.

Rae was rooting for Caroline, partly out of friendship, but more because two pins for Caroline was less scary than two pins for Oliver.

The cameras were waiting in the lodge when the junior chefs arrived.

Chef Nancy covered her mouth. "Oh no! I'm so sorry, Steve. I totally forgot about the interviews."

Steve frowned. "I don't want to go back to the studio at this point. Let's do them in here instead."

Chef Nancy scanned the room and then pointed to one of the armchairs. "What about there? We can start with Oliver. Caroline and Rae can wait at the dining table for their turns."

OLIVER

Who is going to come in second place? Well, it won't be me, because I'm going to win the whole enchilada. I used to think second place would go to Rae, but now I think Caroline has a really good chance.

Second place? Well, Rae is my friend, but Oliver is really good. I think it might be Oliver.

CAROLINE

RAE

Second place is going to be Oliver . . . or Caroline. I don't really understand the question. Why does second place even matter? There isn't a prize!

Rae stomped back to the table and sat down. The interviews weren't fair. They were supposed to be in the closed room with the orange door. Instead, she'd heard every word Caroline and Oliver had said.

Caroline looked worried, and a minute later she was apologizing. "I'm sorry. I was nervous and . . ."

"I don't want to talk about it!" snapped Rae.

Caroline turned and was quiet.

....

After dinner, Chef Nancy led the group back to the school studio. She noticed the silence. What was different? What had happened?

Chef Aimee was waiting with the cameras. "Welcome back, junior chefs. Can you retrieve your desserts from the fridge and set them on the table?"

Caroline made a wish on the way to the fridge: *Let Rae win.* She made another one on the way back: *If not Rae, then let it be Oliver.* That would work too. That way Caroline and Rae would have something to talk about. They could be mad at Oliver together. Together was important! She could win a new whisk pin tomorrow.

"Rolling!" Steve started the cameras.

Caroline glared. This was his fault, him and his tricky questions.

"Desserts!" said Chef Aimee. "What do you think? Isn't this the perfect way to end the day?"

"Yes, Chef."

Caroline turned away from Steve and faced front. Why did everything have to be so complicated? All she wanted to do was keep her best friend and cook.

Chef Nancy arranged the cake samples onto plates.

Chef Aimee studied the desserts. "They're all so different. We have three very distinct chefs, each with her or his own creative vision." She nodded to the junior chefs. "I like that. And I also like the look of these desserts! I can't wait to try them. We'll start with Caroline and end with Oliver. Can you each describe what you made?"

I made a hot chocolate cake with slivered almonds, caramel, and chocolate shavings.

CAROLINE

RAE

I made an apple cream cheese cake with a toasted walnut garnish.

I made a lime cake with strawberry compote, and a fresh strawberry topping with meringue.

OLIVER

"I like the idea of hot chocolate," said Chef Nancy. "But I was expecting spicy. Am I missing something?"

Caroline looked surprised. "It's not that kind of hot. I used a hot chocolate mix to make the frosting."

Chef Aimee scooped up another taste of the frosting. "It's a clever idea, but simple. Why not go the extra mile and add some spice or maybe another flavor, to complement the ones you already have. You need to take this to the next level. I think you could have pushed this a little bit more."

Chef Aimee and Chef Nancy both liked Rae's combination of cream cheese and apples, but Chef Aimee had a problem with the walnut garnish. "It seems a little dry. Candied walnuts might have been a better choice."

Caroline made a third wish, right before Chef Aimee put Oliver's cake in her mouth. *Forget my other wishes. I still want to win. I hope Oliver's cake is horrible!*

Chef Aimee leaned forward. "Oliver, do you have *eight* layers of cake? Remarkable." She tried a bite. "Mmmm—rich and tangy."

"And refreshing," added Chef Nancy. "And I just love the meringue."

Chef Aimee and Chef Nancy moved to the side of the room for a quick discussion. A minute later they were back.

"Oliver, your icebox cake was fabulous; it's visually appealing and palate pleasing. Cold, tangy, sweet—it hits all the right notes. Congratulations, Oliver. Well done. You are the winner of this challenge."

RAE

Watching Oliver get his second pin was not a bonus. Now we're tied in the race for the Golden Envelope. I need that advantage! Caroline and I talked about it right before bed. We have to step it up and be a team. Two against one—one of us has to win this!

CHAPTER 22

C hef Nancy arrived at the breakfast table to a barrage of questions from the three junior chefs.

"Where's breakfast?"

"Why is the table empty?"

"What are we supposed to eat?"

"Wait!" Caroline turned to Rae. "It's another surprise!"

Chef Nancy opened the door. "Let's go. I'll explain at the school studio."

Steve and the cameras were waiting when they arrived.

Chef Nancy gathered the group around the table. "Today's a big day! We have a special guest coming to judge our challenge. It's nice when we can mix things up this way. And I know you'll want the day to go *smoothly*." She smiled mischievously. "You'll want to be filled with energy."

Chef Nancy reached under the table and pulled up a blender.

"SMOOTHIE!" Rae and Caroline both said it together.

"That's right! Our first challenge is a healthy breakfast smoothie including fresh spinach. Spinach is high in protein and fiber. It's a natural superfood that offers benefits to every part of your body. Doesn't that sound like a good start to the day?"

"Yes, Chef."

Chef Nancy tapped the top of the blender. "The pantry will be open for the full five-minute time limit of this challenge. Chef Gary will be in to give the smoothies a taste test, so you'll need two full glasses: one for him and one for you, because your smoothie *will be* your breakfast. Let's get cooking!"

Rae raced to the pantry. If she had to drink a whole smoothie, she definitely wasn't going to make anything too wild. She grabbed spinach, bananas, sugar, and blueberries, and then headed to the freezer.

OLIVER

At home, I drink smoothies at least twice a week. I make them for my mom, too. I could not have asked for an easier challenge. There's this saying: "Make what you know." That's all I have to do.

Oliver filled his blender with banana, fresh spinach, frozen blueberries, yogurt, milk, and almond butter. He hit pulse. Once it was mixed, he'd add his last special ingredient: chia seeds.

Caroline halved an avocado, scooped out the flesh, and mixed it with a banana, fresh spinach, frozen mango chunks, and almond milk. She blended until smooth and then dipped in a spoon to taste. "Ugh." Too sour, too thick, too green! She added sugar, cinnamon, and yogurt and hit pulse.

"ONE MINUTE LEFT!"

Oliver filled up two glasses.

Rae filled up two glasses.

Caroline filled up one and a half glasses, then banged on the bottom of the blender. Her smoothie was too thick; it wouldn't come out. She grabbed a spoon.

"TIME!"

Caroline dropped the spoon and angrily raised her arms. Her smoothie was the opposite of smooth. It was a chunky disaster!

The taste test was over almost as fast as the challenge. Chef Gary was in and out of the studio in just under ten minutes, and half of that time was spent talking about Oliver's smoothie and chia seeds. "Oliver, you added chia seeds! WOW! Did you know that these little seeds are a superfood? They're loaded with antioxidants and are high in protein and fiber. They're very good for your heart." He took another sip of the smoothie. "I like drinking something that is so good for me. Plus it tastes great, too." As soon as his glass was empty, Chef Gary handed Oliver a whisk pin.

"Thank you, Chef." Oliver made a big show of pinning it next to the other two pins on his apron.

Rae scowled. She only had two pins, but poor Caroline only had one!

The winner of the most pins would win an advantage in this week's final elimination round. The competition was stiff as meringue—they needed all the help they could get.

Rae closed her eyes and gave herself a quick silent pep talk. *I can do this! I will win my own food truck!*

I knew I was going to win, so the big surprise for me was Caroline. I thought she'd do a lot better. The pressure of competing really gets to some people. I guess my big competition might be Rae. I'm one pin closer to the Golden Envelope.

OLIVER

"Pretty good." Rae slurped the last bit of smoothie through the straw. "More banana next time."

"That"—Oliver held up his empty glass—"was delicious!"

Caroline choked down half her smoothie and then gave up. "I'd rather be hungry."

CHAPTER 23

Chef Nancy held the door and watched the junior chefs march into the filming studio. The cameras were already rolling.

"Welcome, junior chefs!" Chef Aimee was next to Chef Gary. "Are you ready for your challenge?"

"YES, CHEF!"

"Wow! I like the enthusiasm. As you know, today's challenge involves a special guest: an established famous chef. You'll meet this chef in just a minute, but first I want to tell you how lucky we are. It's a treat for me to be on the stage with him, and it'll surely be a treat for you to meet him."

Steve gave a signal to Chef Gary.

"Okay, junior chefs—it's time to introduce our very special surprise guest! You know him from his innovative recipes: the banh mi donut, the waffle-roasted chicken, the beef pot buns, and now his newest creation: the creatively wrapped egg sandwich—the eggi-gami. Please welcome Chef Anton Margolis, the mash-up king!"

The junior chefs exchanged excited glances and cheered.

Chef Margolis moved next to Chef Gary. "Good afternoon, everyone! I'm very excited to introduce your next challenge. As you know, innovative food ideas take time. No one is expecting you to invent the next culinary craze in just sixty minutes, but that doesn't mean we can't give you a mash-up challenge. Are you ready to test those boundaries?"

"YES, CHEF!"

Chef Aimee held up a red bag. Chef Porter held up a green bag.

"One of these bags contains a card with a food item and the other, a card describing a type of cuisine. You will randomly receive one of each, and these will determine your individual challenge." Chef Margolis reached into the bags, pulled a card from each, and handed them out. Oliver got macaroni and cheese and Italian cuisine; Rae got BLT sandwich and Asian cuisine; and Caroline got chicken nuggets and French cuisine.

"Now, your challenge is to create an innovative appetizer by mashing up your two cards. Use the ingredients of your food item, but you must give it an innovative twist in the style of your listed cuisine." Chef Margolis nodded to Chef Gary.

"Thank you, Chef Margolis. You will have sixty minutes of cooking time for this challenge, not including five minutes of prep time and five minutes in the pantry. There will be three judges tasting your appetizer, so provide samples accordingly. Junior chefs, are you ready?"

"YES, CHEF!"

"CUT."

····

The prep time passed quickly. Chef Nancy made a quick tour of the workstations and then it was time to start again.

"ROLLING!"

The cameras followed the junior chefs into the pantry. There were long shots, and close-ups, but that wasn't the whole story. What the cameras couldn't capture was the feeling of nervous energy.

"TIME!"

Rae dropped her basket onto her worktable. Everything was under control. She had a plan and she had her ingredients, but she was missing something. The *I'm going to win this* feeling. That's what she needed most, and it wasn't going to be in the bottom of her basket.

I'm making a savory version of a macaron. Instead of meringues, I'll have medallions of chicken with a spicy filling.

CAROLINE

RAE

My appetizer is a twist on a fresh roll. It will be a bacon, lettuce, and tomato roll with a tangy mayonnaise dipping sauce.

Right away, I thought of bruschetta. I'm using macaroni and cheese instead of toasted bread.

OLIVER

Chef Margolis raised his hand. "Let's get cooking!"

The junior chefs jumped into action. Sixty minutes would go by fast; every second was valuable. Rae whisked together an egg, salt, dry mustard, and a pinch of sugar, and then in a separate bowl mixed lemon juice and vinegar. Making mayonnaise was tricky—you couldn't rush it. She added half the lemon juice and vinegar to her egg mixture in the food processor and then carefully drizzled in oil as she pulsed the processor until the mixture started to thicken. She added the remaining oil and lemon juice until she had a creamy, thick sauce. "Success! Homemade mayonnaise!" She rushed it to the refrigerator to cool.

Oliver filled a pot with salted water and put it on the stove. Once it was boiling, he'd add the macaroni. Five minutes would probably be enough for the noodles to be just al dente—not too soft, but a little firm to the bite. While he waited, he fried five slices of pancetta and got started on his roux, the base for mostly every good sauce. He melted four tablespoons of butter in a pot, sprinkled it with flour, and whisked to combine. He left the sauce to flip the pancetta and then was back again. Leaving a roux, even for a minute, was a risk. It could burn and stick to the bottom of the pot! He slowly added milk, cooking and stirring until the white sauce was thick and bubbly. Then, he added cream, salt, and pepper, and continued to stir. No worries here. It was perfect.

Caroline thinly sliced two cloves of garlic and mixed them with chopped fresh rosemary and olive oil. She poured almonds onto a cookie sheet, salted them, and put them in the oven to bake.

WHACK! WHACK! She raised the marble rolling pin above her head and struck the chicken breast again. *WHACK!* If Chef Margolis wanted innovation, she was going to deliver. She pushed a round cookie cutter into the first flattened breast and cut out four perfect circles. This was an invention.

....

The first thirty minutes passed quickly and without incident, but that didn't last. Was Chef Gary bad luck? Maybe, because as soon as he started his visits, things started to go wrong.

Chef Gary leaned over the counter next to Rae. "What's that?" He pointed to the strainer in the sink.

"Vermicelli rice noodles for my fresh roll." Rae dipped her tongs into the strainer to pull up a few, but instead ended up with the whole large, gelatinous mass. "OH NO! The noodles fused together!" She dropped the blob back into the strainer and let the tongs fall to the counter. "Now I have to start again." She looked up at the clock. Was there even time? Could she fix what she already had? Chef Gary left her standing at the sink, knife in one hand and a new package of noodles in the other.

Caroline pushed pulse on the food processor twice, then twice more. Chef Gary approached just as she was opening the top. He watched silently. Caroline frowned, dipped a spoon into the almond mixture, and examined it. What? It wasn't crumbs! She'd pulsed too much and now it was flour! Chef Gary slowly backed away. A good chef always found a path out of a mistake. Caroline just needed time to think, but there wasn't any. The minutes were winding down quickly.

Oliver's pan of macaroni and cheese was in the oven. He checked it regularly—every two minutes.

"Mmmm, smells good over here."

"Thank you, Chef. I'm baking a thin layer of macaroni and cheese. When it's firmed up, I'll cut out mini rectangles to use as the base of my bruschetta."

"Very clever. And on top?"

"Pistachio pesto sauce." Oliver held up the bag of pistachios.

Chef Gary looked at the clock, then back at the bag. "Shouldn't you get started? You've got to shell all those pistachios."

"WHAT?" Oliver ripped open the bag and pistachios rolled all over the counter. "I thought these were already shelled!"

Chef Gary returned to the front of the room.

"FIFTEEN MINUTES!"

"Everything going smoothly?" Chef Margolis gave the room a quick scan.

"Mostly." Chef Gary nodded. "You know how it is— there are always a few bumps."

CHAPTER 24

At the five-minute warning, Caroline, Rae, and Oliver were all plating.

Caroline selected the best six nuggets, put her chili mayonnaise into a piping bag, and carefully topped three of the nuggets with a mayonnaise twist. It was the exact consistency she'd hoped for: creamy yet firm. She carefully placed the remaining three nuggets on top and then lined them on edge across the middle of a square plate. Her finishing touch was a decorative drizzle of chili sauce on the side.

Rae pulled her fresh roll wrap from the water, arranged the bacon, fried vermicelli noodles, diced tomatoes, and lettuce on the bottom corner, and rolled. Others might struggle, but she was good at crafts; she had patience. She moistened the sides, folded them in, and then rolled the top to close it. Four minutes left and only one more to go. She cut the fresh rolls in half and arranged three half rolls in the center of the large plate. She added creative swirls of tangy mayonnaise to the side, and a sprinkling of microgreens finished off the presentation.

Oliver generously brushed pistachio pesto over his macaroni bruschetta, added fresh diced tomatoes, and set it on a rectangular board. Two more samples and then a sprinkling of *shelled* salted chopped pistachios over the tops, and he was done.

"TIME!"

Six hands quickly shot into the air.

"CUT."

Chef Gary nudged Chef Margolis. "It's what you've been waiting for. Now we get to taste these amazing creations. Oliver, can you please bring your plate to the table and tell us what you've made?"

Oliver

Oliver walked to the table and set his board down. "I made a brumaca with a topping of pistachio pesto, fried pancetta, fresh tomatoes, and salted pistachios."

Chef Margolis studied the board. "Brumaca? What's that?"

Oliver smiled. It was the exact question he'd been hoping for. "Well, sir, brumaca is a mash-up of bruschetta and mac and cheese. My base is made from baked mac and cheese."

"Well, I have to try this." Chef Margolis picked one up and took a bite. "Crunchy and flavorful. What kind of cheese did you use?"

"A mixture of cheeses, sir. Asiago, fontina, and aged Parmesan."

"I'm impressed. Well done." Chef Margolis popped the rest into his mouth.

Oliver was happy with his review. The judges had used words like *superb, flavorful, creative,* and *sophisticated.*

Caroline was next. She carried her plate slowly up to the front. Why did she always have displays that could tip over? And why hadn't she thought of making up a fancy name like Oliver had? It was too late now.

"I was inspired by French macarons. I made savory chicken nuggets with a sweet chili mayonnaise."

"Brilliant! It's simple but inventive. The best ideas are often the more straightforward ones." Chef Margolis popped a nugget into his mouth.

"I'm having one too!" Chef Gary said.

"Tangy, spicy, and just the right amount of crunch. The breading is very delicate. What did you use?"

"Rosemary-infused almond flour."

Chef Margolis turned to Chef Aimee. "I think I should be worried. I could be out of a job."

Chef Aimee tried the nugget and nodded. "You might be right."

Rae was last. "I made a BLT fresh roll with a tomato and

bacon salsa, crispy vermicelli, lettuce, and a tangy mayonnaise sauce."

Chef Margolis studied the plate. "Beautiful presentation—and quite an impressive design with mayonnaise sauce. I'm guessing you're a visual artist as well."

Rae nodded. "Yes, Chef."

Chef Margolis dipped the fresh roll into the sauce and took a bite. "This has wonderful textures: crunchy and chewy. And the sauce complements the flavors of the salty bacon and the sweet tomatoes. Well done."

Chef Gary liked the bacon salsa, and Chef Aimee said it was much better than a BLT sandwich.

••••

The junior chefs stood in place while the judges moved to the back of the room. Normally they were back in just minutes, but not today. It was taking forever.

Chef Aimee led the way back to the table. "This was a difficult challenge, but I think it might have been even harder for us. You each presented innovative dishes that were creative and flavorful, and the plating was flawless. I know we're about to applaud the winner, but before we do, I'd like to take a minute to acknowledge each and every one of you." The judges all clapped.

Rae blushed, Caroline grinned, and even Oliver smiled.

Chef Aimee turned to Chef Margolis. "Will you make the announcement?"

"Of course. I'd be honored. This was a tightly fought challenge, but the winner had a clear culinary vision and expressed it flawlessly. Caroline, you are the winner of this challenge. Your idea was innovative, fresh, and new. You took an established idea and gave it a creative and sophisticated twist. That kind of genius is rare. Congratulations, Caroline. Please come forward."

I was surprised that Caroline won, but then, she had kind of an advantage. French cuisine isn't much of a challenge for her. Her mom is a French chef. Maybe she wouldn't have done so well if she'd gotten Asian or Italian. I still think mine was more creative. I even made up a new name for my dish.

OLIVER

RAE

I don't feel bad about losing. I did my best. We all did. I think it just came down to preference. Chef Margolis liked Caroline's twist on a dessert item, probably because it's the kind of thing he would do.

I still can't believe I won. Sometimes my brain surprises me—it just comes up with ideas. Can I do it again tomorrow and Thursday? Of course. I have two pins. That's not luck, that's talent.

CAROLINE

R ae shot a quick look at Caroline's apron. Now they both had two pins each. They were tied, and that felt right, but Oliver—he had three! She couldn't let him win. She needed the advantage in the last challenge. There was still time. They were all doing well—anyone could win.

"No cameras," promised Chef Nancy. They were back in the school studio for a quick lesson. "This will just be us, and it will be fast. I know you're all tired."

Rae frowned. No cameras? That meant no surprise challenge, which meant NO PINS! Now she had to wait until tomorrow.

"I want to talk about kitchen lingo. Most of them are idioms." Chef Nancy smiled sneakily. "'Eighty-six the croutons on the salad.' 'How many orders on deck?' 'This taco is dying on the pass!'"

Rae giggled.

Caroline looked confused.

Oliver raised his hand. "Excuse me, ma'am. Is there going to be a test?"

"No, Oliver, there won't be a test, but this might be helpful in a future challenge. I prepared a handout of terms, so you can look it over, for fun. Plus, if you ever work in a restaurant, you'll want to know these. You might even use them in your own food truck."

KITCHEN LINGO AND ITS MEANING

Eighty-six: You have run out of something and it's no longer available on the menu, or you want to take something off the order. "Blueberry pancakes, eighty-six the butter."

In the weeds: You need help. You're behind in your order and you don't know how to catch up. "I'm in the weeds!"

On the fly: The food item is needed right away. Perhaps you sent out a Caesar salad but forgot to add the croutons. The salad will come back and the server will say, "I need croutons on this on the fly."

Mise: Short for *mise en place*. You all know what this means and how important it is to being successful. "My *mise* is ready to go."

On deck: The orders that have been placed and are waiting to be cooked. You might say, "I have two burgers and three pot pies on deck."

Dying on the pass: Food that is prepared and ready to be served, but it's sitting getting cold and not being delivered to the customer. "This chicken is dying on the pass."

SOS: Sauce on the side. "Spaghetti SOS."

All day: This refers to all the food a cook is supposed to cook—the cook's open orders. For clarification a cook may ask, "Can you give me an all day?" The response would be, "You have five salads, three pastas, and one burger all day."

Fire: To start cooking, but with more urgency. "Fire one order of fries!"

Caroline scanned the page. "It's like a whole different language."

Rae made a face. "I wouldn't want to eat anything that died on the pass, and I definitely don't want to be in the weeds."

Caroline agreed. "I hope that doesn't happen to any of us. Eighty-six the weeds!"

Chef Nancy looked at Oliver. "How about you, Oliver? Want to give it a try?"

"Okay, ma'am." Oliver paused, then held out his hand. "New whisk pin on the fly."

Chef Nancy smiled. "Very funny. Eighty-six that. Let's call it a day."

CHAPTER 26

"Yay—real breakfast!" Caroline filled a bowl with cereal. "Eighty-six the smoothie! Two more days and then I don't have to eat this every day."

"I think you're giving it too much credit." Rae chose a cinnamon bun and a bowl of strawberries. "Cereal isn't making you win."

Caroline poured in the milk. "Why take chances? It's good luck."

Oliver watched, chewing on a bagel with lox and cream cheese.

Chef Nancy breezed in. "Good morning, junior chefs. Ready to visit some food trucks?"

Suddenly everyone was excited.

"*Real* food trucks?"

"Do we get to go in them?"

"How many are there?"

She held up her hand. "Let's hold all the questions until we get there."

....

An hour later, they pulled into a bustling parking lot filled with colorful food trucks, overhanging lights, and tented picnic tables.

"There are fourteen trucks in this pod, and each one has a creatively distinct menu. You have fifteen minutes to look around, and then we'll meet up there." She pointed to a big white tent.

Chef Nancy was right; each truck had its own specialty.

Caroline pointed to Meaty Eaty. "That one sells only meat sandwiches, and Waco Taco sells only tacos."

"I thought there'd be more variety in each food truck," confessed Oliver. "You know, like in a restaurant."

Rae looked around. "Look at all the choices. There are fish and chips, pizza, tacos, BBQ, sushi, Indian food, ramen, Korean food, Chinese omelets, sausages, Hawaiian food, noodles, sandwiches, and burgers. If you put them all together, it's like the best restaurant ever!"

Oliver nodded, but he wasn't convinced.

Chef Dorian of the Slider Spot was expecting them, and happily offered a tour. "Just pop your head in and have a look. Just enough room to make the best sliders in town."

It was the shortest tour ever. The space inside the truck was tiny. It was only eight feet wide. There was a counter under the big serving window, and next to a small sink. A mini stove with an oven was on the far back wall, under a stack of shelves crammed with supplies.

Chef Dorian pointed to the driver's seat. "I can get up and go any time I want! It's heaven on wheels!"

....

Chef Nancy met the junior chefs outside the tent. "It's our usual setup. We have your workstations, the pantry, and the table at the front for judging. But there isn't time to look around. Cameras are on and Chef Gary is inside."

"Welcome, junior chefs." Chef Gary waved them closer. "Are you ready to learn more about the food truck biz? After all, one of you will be joining in very soon."

"YES, CHEF!"

"Great! Well, I want to introduce you to a few of the proprietors here at this pod. This is Chef Valentina from Waco Taco, Chef Jenny from Aloha Café, and Chef Phil from Holy Smokes BBQ. They're here to answer your questions. What do you want to know? These are the experts. Who wants to start?"

Oliver raised his hand. "I was wondering: Why do the trucks have such small menus?"

Chef Valentina answered first. "There are many reasons. The kitchen in the food truck is small, so there isn't the room to prepare all kinds of different meals."

"And there's a system," added Chef Jenny. "Many of the items on my menu have similar ingredients, and that's on purpose. I can keep the number of ingredients low and mix and match them to make different dishes."

"And there's the time factor," said Chef Phil. "When someone orders a meal, they don't want to wait around for more than five minutes. I have to deliver the meal fast. My ingredients are prepped and ready to go. So when I get an order all I have to do is cook, plate, and serve."

The chefs had lots of advice. Prepare as much as you can before you open for business. Think about efficiency—can you use your ingredients in more than one dish and use different sauces to spice up your menu? Practice so you'll know where you should store everything. *Mise en place* is crucial for the final assembly of your dishes. And most important, make everything on your menu to the best of your ability. One standout dish is better than three mediocre offerings.

"Wow! Valuable advice. Thank you, chefs!" Everyone clapped. Chef Jenny and Chef Phil waved goodbye, but Chef Valentina stayed right next to Chef Gary.

"Challenge time," whispered Rae.

"I'm ready for it." Caroline's brain was already thinking. Waco Taco was Mexican—that had to be a clue.

Chef Gary leaned forward. "In just a minute we'll go back there." He pointed to the table at the back of the tent. "Chef Valentina is going to give us a lesson on . . ."

She smiled and finished his sentence. ". . . handmade tortillas!"

"Nope, no challenge right now," whispered Rae.

Caroline agreed, but now she had another clue: tacos!

CHAPTER 27

RAE

Corn tortillas are fun and easy to make. It's just three ingredients: masa harina, salt, and hot water. You mix them up until the dough is soft like Play-Doh, not too sticky and not too dry, and then you let it rest in a covered bowl for fifteen minutes. This lets the masa harina absorb the water.

My favorite part was pressing the tortillas in the tortilla press. You roll a small ball of dough until it looks like a Ping-Pong ball. Then you put it in the press and push down with the handle on the lid. Done!

CAROLINE

OLIVER

Tortillas cook fast—only one or two minutes per side on a hot griddle. You have to keep them wrapped up in a kitchen tortilla basket so they stay soft and warm. Fresh tortillas are worth the trouble. They're totally delicious!

"ROLLING."

The first two words out of Chef Gary's mouth were "Taco challenge."

Rae smiled. This was going to be easy. She already knew what to make: smoky pulled pork tacos with a chipotle créma.

Chef Gary paused for a few seconds, then continued. "You have forty minutes to create *two* distinctively different *vegetarian* tacos, and we want you to use fresh vegetables. You may use canned beans without penalty, as there isn't time to make them from scratch. The pantry will be open for the duration of the challenge, so we'll start right from here. Are you ready?"

"YES, CHEF!"

"Let's get cooking!"

Oliver passed Rae on the way to the pantry. She watched him fill his basket with radishes, cilantro, chipotle peppers, onions, tomatillos, mayonnaise, cauliflower, and garlic. How did he have a menu so fast? She took out a pencil and paper.

She had to make a list—it was the only way she could stay organized.

Caroline had one big problem. Cilantro! Wasn't it a staple of Mexican cuisine? Well, not for her. She'd just have to be creative.

I started with the things that take the most time: lentils and sweet potatoes. My lentils are simmering on the stove with cumin and garlic, and my sweet potatoes are roasting in the oven.

RAE

Rae cut a portobello cap into long thin strips, tossed it with olive oil, put it on a tray, and then into the oven. Next up? Grilling corn on the gas burner.

Caroline was busy too. She had two pots on the stove: beans and potatoes. She sliced up two ripe plantains, tossed them with coconut, sugar, cumin, cinnamon, cayenne, and salt, and then added them to the sizzling oil in the hot pan.

Chef Gary came by as she was flipping them over. "Plantains! Now, that's one of my favorites. Smells good. What're they cooking in?"

"Coconut oil, until they're caramelized."

"Good choice, high smoking point. Keep it up."

Chef Gary watched Oliver. What was he doing? He'd

opened the oven twice, moved something inside, tried to add a baking tray, changed his mind, and closed the oven door. Now he was just standing over it with the tray in his hand.

"What's cooking?"

"Not these!" Oliver dropped the tray of tomatillos, garlic, and jalapeños onto the table. "My oven's full—there's no room!"

"What are you making?"

"Roasted vegetable salsa."

"And that's the only choice for roasting?"

Oliver nodded, but then the nod slowly turned into a slow shake. He could use the stovetop.

"Thank you, Chef!"

"For what?" Chef Gary shrugged and turned. "I just asked a question."

Oliver speared two tomatillos on a large fork, turned on the burner, and roasted them over the flame until the skins were brown and blistered. This would take longer than the oven, but the flavor would be worth it.

"TWENTY-FIVE MINUTES!"

"Too soon!" Rae knew she was going to be rushed, but it wasn't supposed to happen this early. She still had to make corn salsa, chipotle créma, and the corn tortillas! Thankfully her *mise en place* was set—that would help. She pulled out the food processor, added sour cream, half and half, chipotle peppers, lime, and salt, and then mixed. She rushed the chipotle créma to the fridge. She made a quick stop in the pantry for one additional item—nasturtium blossoms! They were pretty and had a nice peppery taste. She ran back to her workstation carefully holding the yellow and orange flowers.

Caroline was worried about the mashed potatoes. Could she turn them into potato cakes? Was there time to make her jalapeño compote? She added scallions, lime juice, salt, eggs, and crème fraîche to the potatoes and mixed. Now for the fun part! She scooped out a small spoonful of the mixture, formed it into a patty, and dropped it into a pan of foaming butter. Four minutes on each side and they'd be gold and crispy.

"FIFTEEN MINUTES!"

Creamy chipotle sauce was the last thing on Oliver's list. He whisked mayonnaise, lime juice, puréed charred chipotle peppers, and salt and pepper, then tasted. It was missing something, but what? Creaminess! He ran to the pantry and returned with Greek yogurt.

At the ten-minute mark, everyone was pressing and heating tortillas. At five minutes, they were plating; and when Chef Gary called time, six tired hands rose into the air.

CHAPTER 28

C hef Valentina joined Chef Gary at the front of the tent. The cameras were done with their close-ups of the plates. It was time to judge. Rae felt a shiver slip down her back, Caroline chewed her lip, and Oliver lightly tapped his toes in his shoes. He did it when he was nervous, and from the outside, no one could see.

"Well, that was some fast work. I wasn't sure you were going to make it, but here we are." Chef Gary looked down at the table. "Six amazing tacos. Well done!" He waved his hand. "Please come to the front and stand behind your tray."

Chef Valentina studied the plates with her hands clasped in front of her heart. "What tantalizing tacos! I can't wait to hear about them. Please tell us what you've made."

RAE

I made an ancho chile, portobello, and lentil taco with a tangy garlic-lime slaw and queso fresco. My second taco is a honey-lime sweet potato taco with corn relish, chipotle créma, and nasturtium blossom garnish.

I made a mini green chive potato cake taco with a crème fraîche topping. My second taco is a sweet smashed plantain and bean taco with a spicy jalapeño compote.

CAROLINE

OLIVER

I made a black bean and avocado taco with a radish salsa fresca and feta crumbles. My second taco is a roasted cauliflower taco with a roasted vegetable salsa and creamy chipotle sauce.

Chef Valentina turned to Chef Gary. "I can't believe it. This is amazing. Can we try them now? They all sound incredible!"

"Absolutely! I thought you'd never ask." Chef Gary cut the tacos in half and handed her a fork. "Let's move down the line. We'll start with Rae and her portobello lentil taco."

Chef Valentina took a bite. "The texture is wonderful. I don't think anyone is going to miss the meat with this taco. The mushrooms have a great meaty feel, the lentils add spice, and the avocado tempers the flavor. This slaw is a great tangy finish. I love it!"

Chef Gary winked at Rae. "Well, I don't think there's anything left to say, do you? Sounds like a job well done!"

Rae couldn't stop smiling, especially after the judges tried her sweet potato taco.

"Honey lime is such a great combination. It's a delightful blend of sweet and tangy. This truly is a treat."

"Nice char on the corn, and the chipotle créma is delicious. I love the pop of color from the nasturtiums, plus they add an unexpected peppery accent."

Caroline was next—Rae's glowing reviews made her nervous.

Chef Gary picked up the potato taco. "Potato cake—that's an interesting choice." He took a bite. "Wow, it really works. It has a nice crunchy crust and the flavor is great. I like the addition of scallions."

Chef Valentina licked her lips. "That crème fraîche is a perfect touch."

"That's another win!" Chef Gary winked at Caroline.

The plantain taco was only a half win. Chef Gary liked it, but Chef Valentina thought the jalapeño compote was overpowering. "It covers up the flavor of those marvelous plantains! And they're so special and integral to the dish."

"Oliver!" Chef Gary looked down at the table. "That cauliflower taco looks amazing."

"Radish salsa fresca! That's what I want to try." Chef Valentina took a bite. "Wow. Nice crunchy tang. It really elevates it from ordinary to special."

Chef Gary liked it too, but he liked the cauliflower taco even more. "How did you flavor the cauliflower?"

"With cumin, chili powder, and garlic, Chef."

Chef Valentina nodded. "Your chipotle sauce is a good complement to the roasted salsa. One has a fiery earthiness and the other is smooth and creamy, and the crust of the cauliflower gives this taco a nice crunch."

"Well done, Oliver!" Chef Gary turned to Chef Valentina. "Shall we discuss our findings?"

Caroline, Oliver, and Rae watched the judges walk to the back of the tent. In just minutes, there'd be a winner, and everyone was thinking the same thing: *It could be me.*

CHAPTER 29

RAE

I knew I was going to win the taco challenge! I do my best work when I have a plan. Taking an extra few minutes to think things through at the beginning really helped. The ancho chile, portobello, and lentil taco was a lot of work, but it was worth it. I feel really good about tomorrow. Plus, now I'm even with Oliver—three whisk pins each. It's the best way to go into the final winner-take-all challenge.

The ride in the van back to the lodge was quiet, each contestant thinking their own thoughts. Rae was trying to remember each and every compliment the judges had given her, Caroline was trying to get over being disappointed, and Oliver was angry. Flowers! That's why he'd lost. He wouldn't make that mistake again. If the judges wanted fancy, he'd give them fancy. The next pin would be his. He deserved the food truck and a debut on a real cooking show. Rae and Caroline were worthy competitors. Sure, they'd beaten him in week two, but it wouldn't happen again. Now more than ever, he needed the Golden Envelope. That advantage would ensure his win in the final round.

....

The junior chefs had the afternoon free, and after dinner there was time for video chats with their families. The families were staying in nearby hotels, ready to come to the final challenge tomorrow. Oliver spoke to his parents.

"Thumbs up," said his dad.

"I made schnitzel chicken this week," said his mom, "but you make it better."

Oliver nodded. She missed him.

Caroline's parents were excited about the challenge. They asked questions and listened. The biggest compliment was from her mom. "Trust yourself, Caroline. You don't need any advice from me. I'm so proud of you."

My dad surprised me on the video chat—my grandma is coming to watch the challenge! I can't believe it. She's here! Now everything is even more exciting.

RAE

Chef Nancy gathered the group around the table. "This is our last night together, so I thought we could watch a movie. There's nothing like a good comedy to get everybody relaxed, but . . ." She looked around the room. "We need some snacks."

"Chocolate!"

"Gummy bears!"

"Popcorn!"

"Popcorn! Great idea! Let's go to the school studio and make some."

····

Chef Nancy held the studio door. Oliver stepped in, with Caroline and Rae behind. He stopped. Caroline peered around him. The camera moved in for a close-up. "AAHHH!" Caroline stepped back into Chef Nancy.

Chef Nancy patted her shoulder. "I'm sorry, but it had to be a surprise. It's a surprise challenge."

"So we're not making popcorn?" Oliver looked around the room.

Chef Nancy waved her finger. "The cameras were a surprise, but I didn't lie. We are making popcorn. Let's move to the big table."

Caroline stepped up and followed Chef Nancy. This was her last chance to even the score. If she won this, they'd all go into tomorrow's challenge with the same number of pins. Then there'd have to be some kind of tiebreaker in order to win the Golden Envelope.

Chef Nancy picked a piece of popcorn out of a bowl and held it in her palm. "Why does popcorn pop?"

No hands went up.

"It's water! Each kernel contains a small amount of water, and when the kernel is heated, the water turns to steam and expands. This bursts the shell open, leaving us with this delicious, cooked odd-shaped morsel. A single kernel of popcorn can be launched three feet into the air, so let's keep the lids on the poppers until we're done.

"You have twelve minutes for this challenge. You are to create a bowl of innovative seasoned popcorn. Are you ready?"

"YES, CHEF."

"Let's get poppin'!"

Rae ran straight to the pantry. There wasn't time for notes, but she had an idea—sweet and spicy curried popcorn. She grabbed curry powder, cayenne pepper, turmeric, honey, butter, and salt. "Delicious!"

Oliver had an idea too. Similar, but different—sweet and spicy wasabi. He filled his basket with brown sugar, salt, wasabi powder, cayenne pepper, and butter.

Caroline was the opposite. Her mind was blank—she didn't have a single idea. She stared at the spice wall, hoping for inspiration. And then it happened. She ran back to her workstation with a basketful of spices and a plan: popcorn flavored with herbes de Provence. She mixed rosemary, thyme, oregano, basil, marjoram, fennel seed, savory spice, onion powder, and garlic powder together in a bowl, then set it aside. Now for the popping!

OLIVER

It's really easy to make popcorn, especially with a popper. You put oil in the pot, add kernels, attach the lid, then turn the handle until the popping starts, and keep turning until it stops. After that, I just mixed my seasonings with the melted butter and added them to the popcorn.

"TIME!"

Caroline raised her hands and looked up. Chef Porter was standing next to Chef Nancy.

"Bowls to the front!" Chef Nancy waved the junior chefs forward, and Chef Porter turned her back to the table. "Since our bowls all look the same, this will be a blind taste test. Chef Porter won't know who made what." Chef Nancy switched up the bowls and moved the junior chefs to the side.

Chef Porter turned around. "I bet you didn't know that I was a popcorn person. I've loved it ever since I was a little girl." She tried two pieces of popcorn from each bowl, and then raised her hand. "I like the herbes de Provence—and though it's satisfying, I wouldn't call it innovative. The wasabi popcorn is a little too spicy. I can't imagine eating more than a few pieces. This sweet curry popcorn, though!" Chef Porter reached forward and grabbed a handful. "It's just the right amount of sweet and heat. Delicious. Who made it?"

Rae raised her hand.

"Congratulations, Rae—you are the winner. This popcorn is innovative, interesting, and addictive! I could eat the whole bowl."

"Thank you, Chef!" Rae said an even bigger thank-you when Chef Porter pinned the enamel whisk pin to her apron. Unless the judges had more surprise challenges, she'd won it! The Golden Envelope was hers!

CHAPTER 30

Chef Nancy was happy mixed with a dash of sad. In just a few hours, the three weeks of competition would be over. Saying goodbye to the junior chefs would be hard, but she was proud of each and every one of them. Who would be the winner? She watched them at the breakfast table. It was impossible to guess.

"Big day!" She walked over, clapping her hands. "This is it!"

"After breakfast you'll have a short visit with your families, and then we'll get started. Any questions?"

Steve the producer burst through the door. "The parents are here!"

A second later the room was filled with people.

I was so happy to see my grandma . . . and my dad. I even cried a little bit. Caroline introduced me to her parents. My grandma gave her a big hug. She knows we're best friends now.

RAE

Thirty minutes later Caroline, Rae, and Oliver were following Chef Nancy to the filming studio. She was talking nonstop. "Take your time and plan out your recipes. If you get stuck, take a moment, breathe, and then think of your problem in a new way. Don't be too ambitious. Be aware of your time." She looked back over her shoulder. "Goodness, you all know this already. I guess I'm excited too!"

Chef Nancy pointed to the door. "Before we line up, how about a group high-five? Because whatever happens, we did this together, and this journey has been amazing!"

"And wonderful."

"And special."

"And fun."

That was a surprise. Rae looked at Oliver. He shrugged. "It's true. I had fun."

"ROLLING."

"*Next Best Junior Chef* is proud to announce the final elimination round of this competition." The announcer's voice echoed through the studio. "At the end of today's challenge, we will have our Next Best Junior Chef! They are the best of the best—the cream of the crop. But who will be the

one to rise to the top? Please welcome our three talented contestants: Caroline, Rae, and Oliver!"

Oliver followed Caroline and Rae down the ramp. It was so exciting! The audience was thunderous, clapping and cheering. He puffed out his chest. For a second he didn't notice, but then . . . WHAT! Everything was different. The workstations were gone! The big table was gone! And Chef Gary was standing alone in the center of the room. The only familiar thing was the pantry in the distance.

"Welcome, junior chefs." He pointed to a spot on the floor. "Don't be shy. Come forward, line up here."

Caroline, Rae, and Oliver stood motionless, but their eyes darted around the room, looking for clues.

"As you can see, we've made some changes, and I'm sure you're wondering, *What kind of challenge doesn't need a workstation?*" He raised a finger. "No need to answer, because I'm going to show you . . . right now! Look to your left, because HERE THEY COME!"

Rae screamed.

Oliver's mouth dropped open.

Caroline yelled and flapped her arms.

Three food trucks drove into the studio: the Crafty Café, Bistro Revilo, and Diner Française.

"That's my truck!" Rae shook Caroline's arm. "LOOK! IT'S REAL! It's really real!"

"Oh my gosh! Oh my gosh! Oh my gosh!" Caroline bounced up and down.

Oliver slowly closed his mouth.

RAE

My truck was exactly how I dreamed it would look, only better. It was turquoise with a big round red and yellow Crafty Café logo on the side. My favorite thing was the two big Cs on the very top of the truck—they even spun around!

My truck was amazing! It was silver and shiny like an old-fashioned diner, and it was the only one with a neon sign. It was perfect! The window part that opened for serving had mini flashing lights all around it. I just wanted to hug it!

CAROLINE

OLIVER

My truck was the most sophisticated. It was brown and the logo was tastefully simple—just black and cream. It was a reflection of the kind of food I'm going to make—serious and classy. No gimmicks.

Caroline looked at Chef Gary, then back at the trucks. "THANK YOU! THANK YOU! THANK YOU!"

Chef Gary laughed. "Don't thank me yet. We still have a challenge to do. Are you ready to hear about it?"

The junior chefs forced themselves to look away from the trucks. "YES, CHEF!"

"Don't worry, they aren't going anywhere. You'll have plenty of time to explore. The trucks might look different on the outside, but inside they're all the same. Just like the Slider Spot food truck you saw on your field trip, they each have an oven, stove, sink, cooking supplies, and of course limited counter space. The winner of *Next Best Junior Chef* will of course get to keep their food truck, so we're asking you to test them out. This is it! The final challenge, so don't hold back. Show us what you can do! We will be judging you on your performance in this final challenge, but will also consider all of the wonderful dishes you've created in the past three weeks.

"Now, your challenge is to prepare an entrée, a side dish, and a dessert that you would serve out of your food truck. There will be ninety minutes for this challenge, not including five minutes of prep time and five minutes in the pantry. The pantry will remain open for the duration of the challenge, due to your limited counter space. So, are you ready?"

"YES, CHEF!"

"OH! Almost forgot!" He waved the Golden Envelope. "Who gets the advantage?"

Rae raised her arm. The four whisk pins were neatly aligned and twinkling on her apron.

"Please open it and read it aloud."

Rae pulled out a card. "Congratulations, you get first pick of a partner for this challenge, and you may pick the partners for the other two competitors." She frowned. Partner?

She scanned the audience, looking for Tate. Was he coming? He waved, but didn't move. She turned back to Chef Gary. Chef Aimee and Chef Porter were joining him, and they were wearing aprons.

Chef Gary quickly put one on too. "It's us! We're the partners! We're excited to be your helpers in this challenge, *but* there are limits. We are line cooks only! We will not tell you what or what not to do. We're just helping hands!" He wiggled his fingers.

Rae shuffled nervously. This wasn't going to be easy, being in a small space with a famous chef.

Chef Gary grinned as he looked over the shocked faces of the junior chefs. "Okay, Rae, time to choose."

I'm really lucky that Rae gave me Chef Aimee. She's so easy to be around. Rae probably picked Chef Gary because he's fun and funny. He'll probably make a lot of jokes. I knew Oliver was going to get Chef Porter. That was smart. Just having her in my truck would make me nervous.

CAROLINE

Five minutes wasn't much time to create and organize three entirely different dishes, but the junior chefs weren't amateurs anymore. After three weeks of intense training, they were professionals.

RAE

I'm going to win because I have a clear understanding of what I want my food truck to be. I'm not just making lunch or dinner—I'm using food to bring people together to be excited about being creative and expressing themselves. There'll be crafts for the hands and food for the soul.

I'm going to win because Bistro Re-vilo is a revolutionary idea—locally sourced food and a sophisticated menu. I'm not just going to offer three or four things on the menu. I'm going to be like a real restaurant. I don't need to be part of a pod; my food truck can stand alone.

OLIVER

CAROLINE

I'm going to win because diner food and French food is a great mash-up. I won the mash-up challenge, and that has made me more confident in my vision. My food reflects who I am: French and American and a chef with a passion for great inventive food.

The producer lined up the junior chefs across from the judges next to the pantry. "We'll start here for the pantry run, and when it's over, run to your truck and stand in front."

"ROLLING!"

"Are you ready for the pantry run?"

"YES, CHEF!"

Rae stole a quick look into the bottom of her basket. Her list was there—she was ready.

Chef Gary raised his hand. "GO!"

Rae had a plan. Dessert first, because it needed to set in

the fridge. Then she'd ask Chef Gary to do some prep work. Would it be weird? Probably—it was hard to imagine telling Chef Gary what to do. But she didn't have time to think about that now. She ran to the produce section, picked strawberries, figs, and fresh spices, and then moved to the baking section.

Caroline ran into the pantry, with Janet the camerawoman following closely behind. Caroline grabbed potatoes, leeks, and broccoli rabe. When Caroline went to the fridge, Janet switched over and followed Oliver. He had steaks, brussels sprouts, pecans, anchovies, and red wine vinegar in his basket. He stopped at the spice shelf and added vanilla, paprika, garlic, onion, coriander, dill, red pepper flakes, salt, and pepper. His steak rub was going to be amazing.

The five-minute pantry run was over too fast. Caroline was glad the pantry was going to stay open throughout the challenge. Her basket was overflowing, but she'd definitely need to go back for more supplies. She waited in front of her food truck, happy for the extra time. What job should she give Chef Aimee? Pound pork chops or clean potatoes? And how would she keep her busy for ninety minutes? Was there really that much to do?

Chef Gary and Chef Nancy walked to the center of the room. "Chef Nancy is going to be the time keeper for this event." Chef Gary smiled, adjusted his apron, and walked toward Rae. The cameras moved in for close-ups of the junior chefs standing with their helpers. Oliver offered Chef Porter his hand and they shook like real partners. Rae looked up at Chef Gary. She should have thought of that. Too late now— it would just look like she was copying, so instead she just smiled.

"Are you ready, junior chefs?"

"YES, CHEF!"

"Are you ready, helpers?"

"Yes, Chef."

Chef Nancy raised her hand. "Let's get COOKING!"

Oliver ran to the door of the food truck, opened it, and froze. The space was smaller than he'd remembered. Where could he put Chef Porter so she wasn't in the way? He stepped up, looked around, and decided on the little counter in the far corner next to the sink. The most important thing was counter space; he needed it all for himself.

Chef Aimee is so nice. I was really nervous, but she made a joke about being like a sardine, and that calmed me right down. I gave her two jobs— first make cereal milk, then pound pork chops—and I got started on cutting up figs for my fig jam. Having an extra pair of hands is going to be a real help.

CAROLINE

CHAPTER 32

OLIVER

I'm making stacked mini steaks with herbed anchovy butter, Parmesan brussels sprouts, and for dessert, pecan shortbread cheesecake with salted caramel. I picked as many locally sourced items from the pantry as I could find, because that's important to me.

I'm making chicken-fried pork à la croque-monsieur, pan-fried fingerling potatoes with leeks, and cereal milk pot de crème for dessert. I wanted to make croissants, but you need more than ninety minutes to make the pastry.

CAROLINE

RAE

I'm making broiled chicken tenders three ways, tri-flavored grilled corn, and roasted strawberry parfaits with lemon and basil creams. It will be sort of a mix and match—I'll give the customer choices and they can choose which sauce they want for their chicken.

"What next?" Chef Gary brushed off his hand on his apron.

Rae was surprised; he was a fast worker, maybe too fast. He'd already chopped garlic, cilantro, parsley, shallots, basil, and mint, and pitted and chopped green olives. What was next was a good question.

She pointed to the bowls of freshly made lemon and basil creams. "Are you allowed to take things to the fridge?"

"Absolutely." Chef Gary picked up the bowls and stepped out the door.

Rae wanted to say "Take your time," but you probably couldn't do that. Knowing Chef Gary he'd be back in thirty seconds. And then what? She looked at her list—slicing and grating. She sighed, relieved to have a plan. Busy Chef Gary was fine, but Chef Gary just watching what she was doing made her anxious. She spread her granola mixture on a baking tray, put it in the oven, and set the timer for twenty minutes.

····

Since Chef Porter was by the sink, Oliver gave her a cleaning job. Wash and trim the brussels sprouts. His shortbread crust was in the oven, and it smelled delicious.

Chef Porter glanced over.

He nodded. "I'm going to make the cheesecake."

She nodded back.

He normally didn't give a play-by-play of what he was doing, but the silence was awkward. He was glad when Chef Porter turned on the water—that meant she was busy. He could focus on the cheesecake. He put cream cheese and sugar into the food processor, mixed, scraped down the sides, and then added the first egg. The noise of the mixer made it impossible to talk. Too bad he couldn't run it for the next hour.

OLIVER

I'm pretty serious and focused while I'm working. I don't usually talk, but the quiet was making me nervous. It was really uncomfortable. So I asked Chef Porter, "What's the best sandwich you've ever had?" Turns out it was roast beef and aged cheddar— she ate it on top of a mountain in the snow. And that's how we found out that we both love cross-country skiing and animals. We don't get snow at home, but every winter we go to Colorado to visit my uncle. That's where I learned to ski.

"THIRTY-FIVE MINUTES!" yelled Chef Nancy.

Chef Aimee pointed to the counter. "My *mise* is ready to go. Can I start?"

Caroline stopped stirring the figs and double-checked the setup: pork, egg mixture, and flour. "Yes—go!"

Chef Aimee dipped the first pork chop into the egg mixture, dredged it in flour, and then transferred it to a wire rack.

Caroline pulled the broccoli rabe from the oven and then carefully placed a roasting pan on the rack. This was tricky; the roasting pan held four ramekins filled with custard resting in water. She held her breath until the pan was securely on the rack, and then she loosely covered the ramekins with foil, closed the oven door, and set the timer.

"That's going to be a tasty custard. What next?" Chef Aimee pointed to the completed pork chops.

"Wash the potatoes?"

"I'm on it." Chef Aimee emptied the fingerling potatoes into a strainer and turned on the water.

Rae pulled her pan of granola from the oven. "Next up, the hot green relish."

"Sounds good and spicy. What can I do?" said Chef Gary.

Rae handed him a mortar and pestle. "Bash the garlic and salt."

"Bashing—is that an official Rae term?"

"Well, maybe if I'm mad."

Chef Gary raised his hand in mock fury, tossed a peeled garlic clove into the bowl, and smashed it. "Ahhhh!"

Rae laughed. Chef Gary was a fun helper.

RAE

I talk to myself a lot. Some people probably find it annoying, but it's working really well with Chef Gary. I'll just talk and he answers or says something funny. I'm not nervous at all. I like watching him work; he's good at everything. If Tate was Master Chopper, Chef Gary is the Conqueror of the Kitchen.

CHAPTER 33

Did you hear it? Chef Nancy just said TWENTY minutes!"

Chef Aimee stepped forward and patted Caroline on the arm. "Don't worry, we'll get it done."

Caroline counted off on her fingers. "We still have to assemble the pork chops, cook the potatoes, make whipped cream, and assemble the dessert."

Chef Aimee leaned over the stove and stirred the potatoes. "These look done to me. Fire the pork chops! Now only three things left."

When the pork chops were finished frying, Caroline placed them on a baking sheet, spread them with fig compote, added a slice of fontina cheese and the cooked broccoli rabe, and then spooned on the béchamel sauce. She looked around for the other cheese. Where was the comté cheese? She called to Chef Aimee. "Grated comté on the fly, *s'il vous plaît!*"

A minute later, a bowl of grated cheese was in her hands.

Caroline sprinkled the comté over the béchamel sauce. "Thank you, Chef Aimee—that was perfect timing. Now they're ready for the oven."

Oliver and Chef Porter were working on the brussels sprouts. She was putting on the coating, Oliver was frying them, and they were talking. Oliver couldn't believe it— Chef Porter had once ridden a horse right next to a buffalo. That trumped his bald eagle carrying a salmon, but she didn't agree. "You were lucky to see such a wonder of nature. It must have been amazing."

"What's that smell?" Oliver dropped the spatula and opened the oven. The cheesecake! He looked at the timer on the stove—oh no, he'd forgotten to set it! With so much going on, that was a crucial mistake.

"Oh, dear!" Chef Porter peered into the oven. "Perhaps it's not that bad."

Oliver pulled it out and set the dark brown mass on the counter. It was obvious; there was no salvaging it.

"Brussels sprouts!" shouted Oliver. He turned back to the stove, scooped out the remaining four, and set them on paper towels to drain.

Chef Porter glanced up at the clock. "Thirteen minutes, Oliver. What's left to do?"

"Fire the steaks, plate, *AND* make a whole new dessert!"

He looked up and apologized. "I'm sorry, Chef. I just really wanted to win."

"Of course you do," said Chef Porter. "So don't give up! You've made a lovely salted caramel sauce, you have chocolate and . . ." She raised her eyebrows.

"And, and, and." He repeated the word and looked around. Ten minutes! What could he make in ten minutes? His eyes stopped on the mini microwave.

A second later he was gone, off to the pantry for supplies.

OLIVER

Chef Porter made me make it happen. I'm lucky she was helping me. I don't normally use a microwave, but this was an emergency. I greased a mug, mixed flour, sugar, cocoa, and salt and then added an egg, milk, oil, and vanilla, and mixed again. I topped it with chocolate and put it in the microwave and set the timer for ninety seconds. It was a miracle. I even had time to make two more.

"FIVE MINUTES!"

Caroline filled a piping bag with mustard sauce and swirled a design on the edge of her plate. She pulled a pork chop from the oven, set it down on one side, and arranged fingerling potatoes on the other. She added freshly chopped parsley on the potatoes. The dessert was easy. All she had to do was top off the custards with whipped cream and a sprinkle of crushed sugared cereal.

Chef Gary watched Rae wipe off the counter and pick out a plate. "Can I help?"

She shook her head. Plating was important. It was the *ta-da* moment for the customer.

She stacked the broiled chicken tenders in the center of the plate and filled three mini dishes with her two relishes and one sauce. The customer would be able to mix and match any way they wanted. They could craft their own meal!

Next up was the corn. She grabbed a cutting board, created three long stripes using the seasonings for the corn, then rolled the buttered corn over the top.

Success! She placed the striped corn next to the chicken.

"Dessert?" Chef Gary pointed to the glass jar filled with roasted strawberries, granola, and cream.

Rae smiled and added a mint leaf.

Oliver stacked five mini steaks on his plate, adding a pat of colorful anchovy butter between each layer, and one on top. He added a smear of spicy mayonnaise to one side of the plate and fanned out five brussels sprouts on the other. He drizzled caramel sauce on the mug cake and topped it off with shaved chocolate as a garnish.

"TIME!"

"Congratulations!" said Chef Aimee.

"Nicely done," said Chef Porter.

Chef Gary gave Rae a high-five.

CHAPTER 34

Caroline, Oliver, and Rae brought their plates out to the large table in the center of the room, and then stood off to the side while the cameras took close-ups of the food.

"How did it go?" whispered Caroline.

"Fantastic! Chef Gary is so nice!"

"Me too. I really like Chef Aimee."

"Chef Porter." Oliver shook his head.

Uh-oh, thought Caroline.

Oh boy, thought Rae.

Oliver smiled. "Chef Porter is my favorite!"

"JUNIOR CHEFS!" Steve the producer waved his hand. "Please come to the table and line up behind your plates."

The judges lined up on the other side with the three chefs from the food trucks, and as soon as everyone was in place, Chef Gary led the group in a round of applause. "This is for you! Because you're here and we're proud of you!" The audience joined in. It was thunderous. Rae looked for her grandma, and found her right next to Caroline's parents, clapping and waving.

Chef Gary raised his hands to quiet the crowd. "As you can see, we have some special guests up here. So let me introduce them. We have Chef Valentina from Waco Taco, Chef Jenny from Aloha Café, and Chef Phil from Holy Smokes BBQ. These fine chefs were very generous with their time, helping our junior chefs learn all about the food truck business. So of course we wanted them here for this special challenge. Thank you, all of you, for coming." Chef Gary and the audience clapped again, but this time Chef Gary did not have to raise his hands for quiet. Chef Gary scanned the faces of the junior chefs. "Are you ready to get started?"

"YES, CHEF!"

He nodded. "Okay, let's do it. Caroline, why did you choose these dishes for your Diner Française menu?"

"My chicken-fried pork à la croque-monsieur is inspired

by chicken-fried steak. I love American diners, but I don't always like the food. I want people to have that fun diner experience, but with a more interesting menu. I am half French and half American, so I'm a mash-up too. Instead of french fries or mashed potatoes, I made fingerling potatoes with leeks, and my dessert is a cereal milk pot de crème with a crushed cereal garnish."

Chef Gary looked to Chef Aimee. "And how was Caroline's working style?"

"It was just like Caroline: diligent, organized, and creative."

Chef Gary cut the food into small bites, to share.

"Delicious!"

"Flavorful!"

"Decadent."

But not everyone liked the pork.

"Too rich."

"Somewhat salty."

"A little greasy."

Caroline was hoping for unanimous love, but still, the potatoes and dessert were a hit.

Chef Gary thanked Caroline, and then nodded to Rae. "Rae, why did you choose these dishes for your Crafty Café menu?"

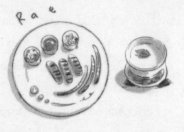

"I want to introduce people to how ingredients can be used in different ways. I'm interested in giving people the tools to craft their own meals. They can mix and match and be creative. I made broiled chicken tenders, because it's familiar, but I paired it with three adventurous sauces. I made a hot green relish with olives, a balsamic fig relish, and honey pepper sauce. My tri-corn has a lime topping, a mint feta topping, and a basil topping. My favorite thing about eating is trying new things, and I offer that to my customer. For dessert, I made a roasted strawberry parfait with lemon and basil creams."

Chef Gary nodded. "I've seen Rae in action, and she is something. She has a creative, passionate spirit."

Visually, everyone agreed, the tri-corn was genius. Rae crossed her fingers while the judges tried the food.

"Inventive."

"Astounding!"

"Addicting."

But two of the judges didn't like the dessert.

"Complex and confusing."

"Too many flavors."

When the judges were done, Rae couldn't do anything but smile.

Chef Gary thanked her and moved on to Oliver. "Oliver, why did you choose these dishes for your Bistro Revilo menu?"

"Yes, Chef. My idea is to bring locally sourced bistro food to the people. Not everyone can afford to go to a fancy restaurant, or even feel comfortable in that kind of environment. I want to introduce people to new options and new ideas about food. Food is something that should be appreciated and savored. It should be a joy. I made mini stacked steaks with an herbed anchovy butter and Parmesan brussels sprouts. I changed my dessert, so now it's a chocolate mug cake with a salted caramel topping."

Chef Gary turned to Chef Porter. "Any words to share about Oliver?"

"Oliver is a determined, serious chef and an impressive problem-solver."

Everyone liked Oliver's steak.

"Rich."

"Satisfying."

"Amazing!"

The brussels sprouts were not as successful.

"Undercooked."

"Bitter."

"Bland."

But the dessert was loved, especially the salted caramel topping. It was more than Oliver was expecting, but he couldn't get over the comments about the brussels sprouts. Would they be his downfall?

Chef Gary took a moment to study the junior chefs. Then he turned to the cameras. "Our young chefs did an amazing job today. Let's all thank them." The audience burst into applause. Once everyone was settled down again, he had one last statement.

"This is not going to be an easy decision."

CHAPTER 35

Caroline studied her food truck. It was better than she'd even imagined, and even though they'd only just met, she was in love.

The judges were out of sight, but not out of mind. What were they saying? Who were they fighting for? Rae, Oliver, or Caroline?

Caroline fidgeted with her fingers, Oliver tapped his toes, and Rae played with her necklace. It was hard to wait.

"They're coming back!" Caroline nudged Rae. You couldn't tell what someone was thinking by watching them walk, but Caroline studied the judges, hoping for a clue.

Chef Gary nodded to the junior chefs. "I'm sorry for the long wait, but this was an important and extremely hard decision to make. We had to get it right. It has been a privilege to get to know each one of these young talented chefs over the past three weeks. There have been some ups and downs, but regardless, they have had their eye on the prize and delivered one hundred percent." He gestured toward the food trucks. "This challenge today was not easy. It was about more than food—it was also about innovation and ideas and efficiently managing the production of three different dishes in a confined space. We are very proud of each and every one of you.

"Caroline, you have a culinary confidence that is well beyond your years. Rae, you are passionate, daring, and remarkably creative. Oliver, you are determined, steadfast, and extremely talented. We are honored to be here with you now."

Chef Gary took a moment to look each junior chef in the eye. He smiled, but then a minute later looked serious. "This part is never easy. After careful consideration of this challenge and reviewing the past three weeks of competition, we have two contestants vying for the top, which means we will have to ask one of you to hang up your apron."

He looked over the group, then settled his gaze on Caroline. "Caroline, we have enjoyed having you on the show. You have delighted us with your culinary talent, and I have

THE WINNER IS . . .

no doubt that we will be hearing from you again. Unfortunately, you are not in the top two. I'm sorry, Caroline—I have to ask you to hang up your apron."

Caroline nodded. "Thank you, chefs. This was the greatest experience of my life. I won't ever forget it!"

Rae watched her take off her apron and walk toward the door. She was numb. Caroline was leaving? For the moment, it was bigger than anything else.

I kind of knew my review wasn't as good as Rae's and Oliver's, but I wanted that food truck so bad! I was just hoping I was wrong. I didn't know how much I wanted the prize until I saw it. So in the end I'm even more motivated than before. I believe in myself—I can still do it! I'll get my own truck—just not on this show.

CAROLINE

Chef Aimee stepped forward. "Now we are down to two extremely talented chefs, and really, they are both deserving, but we had to choose only one to earn the title of Next Best Junior Chef." She nodded apologetically.

Rae couldn't move. She felt sick, excited, nervous, and scared all at the same time. Was there a word for that? Was Oliver feeling it too? She stared at Chef Aimee, forcing herself to concentrate.

Oliver stood tall and confident. Even his toes were still. He wanted this. He deserved it. He was going to get it. There were only two words he was waiting to hear: *Congratulations, Oliver.*

Chef Aimee continued. "Our winner consistently displays a grasp of technical skill but always adds a creative spin. This chef is spirited but compassionate. A master of plating, this chef is not afraid to try new things. Over the last three weeks, this chef has exhibited a keen interest in learning culinary techniques out of their comfort zone.

"We have no doubt that this desire for knowledge will continue. Standout dishes have included a stunning honeycomb pie crust, *alfajores,* black cod with morel sauce, unicorn donuts, and innovative ancho chile, portobello, and lentil vegetarian tacos. Our winner of today's challenge and the title of Next Best Junior Chef is . . ."

Rae was numb. She'd been numb ever since Chef Aimee had said the words *pie crust.* All the amazing, wonderful things Chef Aimee had just said—they were about *her!*

"RAE!! Congratulations, Rae. Please come to the front!"

The crowd erupted, yelling, screaming, clapping. Rae looked up and found her grandma and dad, their hands in the air. It was like a dream! She was in it, but watching, too. The wave of excitement pushed her up to the front next to Chef Aimee. Chef Nancy helped her with a new apron—the

one only champions could wear. Rae moved her hand up to feel the embroidery—the raised words that spelled *Next Best Junior Chef* and then underneath, her name. And suddenly her dream was real. The clapping got louder, confetti poured from the stage light bar above, and everything came into focus. There was Oliver across from her, the judges next to her, and up in the stands—her best friend, Caroline, jumping up and down and cheering.

OLIVER

Of course I'm disappointed. I guess I had more to learn than I thought I did, so I'll keep trying. I'm not the kind of person who gives up. If this experience makes me a better chef, then it was all worth it. Bistro Revilo *will* be a reality.

I can't believe I'm standing here in my very own food truck! I keep saying the same two words over and over again. It's real! It's real! Not everyone gets to have a dream come true, so I know I'm really lucky. This truck is everything I wanted. I can't wait to get cooking! I even had a new great idea—guest chefs. I have a list, but I'm saving it as a surprise. I've kind of decided . . . I like surprises.

RAE

"Thank you for watching this exciting conclusion of *Next Best Junior Chef.* The journey is just starting for Rae, our new Next Best Junior Chef, and the first stop is Chef Gary Lee's award-winning show *Adventures in Cooking*! How will she fare in Italy, the land of pesto, pasta, and pizza? Will this junior chef keep up with Chef Gary? Is she up for the challenge? You'll just have to watch to find out . . ."

Chef Gary pointed to an empty plate. "What shall we make for lunch? How about something long and stringy?"

"I love pasta!" Rae nodded eagerly. Pasta was easy.

Chef Gary reached under the counter, pulled up three large whole squids, and dropped them onto a cutting board.

The camera moved in for a close-up. Rae grimaced and squirmed uncomfortably.

"What?" Chef Gary exaggerated his confusion. "You've never cut these up?"

Rae shook her head and tried to look brave. Then all of a sudden she jumped back and gasped. One of the tentacles moved!

MISS EPISODES ONE AND TWO?

Press rewind and treat yourself!

How to Cook Flavorful Food

from *The Young Chef: Recipes and Techniques for Kids
Who Love to Cook* by the Culinary Institute of America

. . . .

Making delicious food involves choosing ingredients that taste great together. This can be accomplished by combining foods' flavors and textures in different ways.

How We Taste

Taste Buds

When you look at the surface of your tongue in the mirror, you will see that it is covered in little bumps that are called papillae fungiform. These delicate bumps contain taste buds and temperature receptors that interact with the compounds found in food. These cells immediately send the taste information to our brain, where we interpret the information and make decisions about how we think the food tastes. The average person has more than ten thousand taste buds. Because kids have more taste buds on their tongues than adults, they are better tasters. Luckily, taste buds regenerate every couple of weeks, but after age forty this regeneration slowly decreases. The five primary tastes that our taste buds detect are sweet, sour, salty, bitter, and umami.

But flavor is a complex sensation produced by more than just taste—it's a combination of taste and aroma.

Bitter
Salty
Sour
Sweet

Taste + Aroma = Flavor

The nose contains olfactory receptors, which are cells that send aroma information to the brain. When we chew food, chemicals are released and rise up from our mouths into our nostrils, triggering the olfactory receptors. Our brains then process the information from the taste buds and olfactory receptors to create the true flavor of the food.

When you lose your sense of smell, it limits flavor and therefore also limits your desire to enjoy food. If you've had allergies or a cold, then you might have noticed this loss of flavor when your nose was stuffy.

Creating Flavors in Food

When you cook, you create depth and dimension by varying the proportions of the five primary flavors as you decide what ingredients to use. Each individual taste interacts with other tastes by either complementing or contrasting their basic characteristics.

Here are some common ingredients that reflect each of the five primary tastes:

Sweet Ingredients

- Fruits
- Ketchup
- Sugar
- Honey
- Chocolate
- Syrups
- Jams and jellies
- Barbecue sauce

Sour Ingredients

- Citrus
- Vinegar
- Yogurt
- Sauerkraut
- Pickles
- Sour cream

Salty Ingredients

- Salt
- Cured meats like bacon and salami
- Soy sauce
- Cheese
- Snack foods like chips, nuts, and pretzels
- Olives

Bitter Ingredients

- Arugula
- Coffee
- Kale
- Grapefruit
- Bitter chocolate
- Horseradish
- Watercress

Umami-Rich Ingredients

- Steak
- Fermented foods like miso paste
- Soy sauce
- Mushrooms
- Tomatoes
- Aged cheeses like Parmesan
- Cured foods like cured ham
- Celery
- Green tea
- Seaweed

Complementing flavors are similar flavors that blend well. Think of making a fruit salad. All of the individual fruit flavors are delicious on their own, but they are all bright, fresh, sweet, and a little acidic, so they also blend together well. Or think of mushroom gravy with roast beef and mashed potatoes. All of these flavors are warm, rich, and earthy. They all complement one another because of their similarities.

When opposite—*contrasting*—flavors and textures are combined and eaten together, they support each other and create a unique and appealing eating experience. There are many examples of this in the foods we eat every day:

- Peanut butter + jelly = rich and creamy with sweet and salty
- Hot dog + relish, mustard, or sauerkraut = salty and fatty with sweet and sour
- Crème brûlée = rich and creamy with sweet, crispy, and caramelized
- Kettle corn = crispy, salty, and sweet
- Fried fish + tartar sauce = crispy and fatty with sour

Building Flavor Through the Use of Aromatic Ingredients

Aromatics are flavorful ingredients used to begin the cooking of many of our favorite dishes. They are called aromatics because they bolster the flavor and aroma of a dish. Onions, garlic, celery, carrots, ginger, peppers, tomatoes, and spices are often cooked as the first step of a recipe in order to "build" flavor. Onions and garlic are two of the most commonly combined foods in the kitchen. They can serve as the main flavoring (for example, onion soup), but more often they are used as foundational aromatic and flavoring ingredients. They add depth of savory flavor as well as sweetness.

There are two ways to cook aromatics:

Sweating means to cook them over low heat so that the moisture in the food is slowly released without the food turning brown.

Browning occurs at higher heat, when the sugars in the food heat up and caramelize. This will develop the flavor as well as the texture of the aromatics, releasing sweet flavors from the sugars and sometimes creating a crispy outer edge. When browning garlic in particular, it is best to heat it slowly over low heat so it does not become bitter.

Seasoning

The process of **seasoning** involves adding an ingredient to give foods a particular flavor. Common seasonings include salt, pepper, herbs, spices, and condiments. To season "to taste" means to taste the food as you add the seasonings and stop when the food tastes best to you.

Building a Vocabulary to Describe Flavor and Texture

These words are commonly used to describe foods' tastes and textures. Learning these words will help you communicate the language of food. What are some other words you might use to describe food?

Sweet: Sugary, Syrupy

Sour: Tangy, Tart, Acidic

Bitter: Harsh, Acrid

Salty: Over-salted

Fatty: Oily, Buttery, Greasy, Slippery

Starchy: Floury, Gluey, Granular

Pungent: Overpowering, Heady, Strong, Spicy

Spicy: Hot, Piquant, Peppery, Fiery, Zesty

Fruity: Tropical, Fresh, Floral, Citric

Chemical: Metallic, Ammonia, Soapy

Rancid: Putrid, Foul, Off, Sour, Spoiled

Coarse: Grainy, Rough

Thick: Gooey, Gelatinous

Smooth: Soft, Creamy

Creamy: Smooth, Buttery, Silky, Soft

Crispy: Crackly, Hard, Crunchy

Hard: Firm, Ridged